BLOOD TIES

Unique Penn

PROLOGUE

"Wake up bitch!"

Jaleesa moaned in pain as ice cold water was thrown on her naked, lacerated skin. It felt like Chinese torture. She couldn't tell what time it was, what day it was, or where she was. She could barely remember how she'd gotten to this place. She'd been drugged and kidnaped by two thugs who kept insisting she knew where her best friend Tasha's uncles Raymond and Charles could be found.

It was confusing to say the least; in the beginning they kept insisting she was someone who she was not, her best friend, Tasha. They had bound her hands, feet and mouth with duct tape, and she was tied to a dining room chair in what seemed like someone's basement that had been dry walled and apparently sound proofed to her chagrin. Jaleesa's face felt like it was on fire. The pain in her left eye had become unbearable. It had begun to swell from the butt of the gun to the side of her face, for spitting in one of the gun men's faces, hence the duct tape on her mouth.

"Yo, take the tape off her mouth." The taller of the masked men said to the other.

"Now look shorty, I'm only going to ask you one more time where your Uncle Raymond is." He said menacingly. "The time for games is over. You still got a chance to live little mama, you haven't seen either of our faces, just say the address and we'll let you go. Hell, we'll even drop you off at a hospital."

As the shortest of the pair reached out and snatched the tape from Jaleesa's mouth, she considered making up any address just to get away from this torture. She had no idea where the twins laid their head and was relieved at this point that she didn't. She would have

3

broken hours ago if she did, and she knew that. The thought saddened her, because the twins were like her uncles, just not blood related. A vicious slap to the face shook Jaleesa out of her reflection.

"Shorty are you gonna answer, or is this the end of the line for you? Think long and hard before you answer, these might just be your last words."

When Jaleesa looked into the soulless eyes boring into her from the other side of that mask, she knew that she had no chance in hell of ever leaving this place alive, whether she'd seen their faces or not. A quick prayer raced through her mind and as a tear fell down her face, she thought they may have broken her body, but they wouldn't break the loyalty she had to the Johnson family. For decades, they had held her family down and vice versa, she could never betray them. If she died tonight, she knew Raymond and Charles would kill whoever had done this to her. Although she wanted to survive this situation, the odds were not in her favor, so she answered accordingly.

"Even if I did know where they were, I would never tell you, but I will tell you this, the twins are going to slaughter you and your friend. You will have to live in fear every minute, of every day of your recently shortened lives. Fuck you!"

The taller of the two took his mask off, much to the objection of the shorter man. "What you doing man, don't let her see your face!" He said nervously.

When the taller of the two pulled his mask off Jaleesa felt urine running down her leg. She knew this was the end of the road for her. She knew this nigga, had kicked it with this nigga, and now he came to kill her. She had been set up for the dummy. The devilish smile on the gunman's face said it all.

4

"Goodnight bitch!" He said with so much venom you knew he had a personal vendetta against her. With that he pulled the trigger.

As Jaleesa was enveloped in darkness, her last thoughts were, "That bitch Kristen..."

CHAPTER 1

Mothers

It was hot that summer in Chicago, in more ways than just temperature. It was especially hot on Chicago's notorious Southside, in the Roseland community. For some reason, there had been an increase in gang activity, drug dealing, and turf wars that increased the homicide rate significantly. Add to that a decline in home ownership, quality education, community involvement, and the extreme heat that causes so many black people to lose their mind in the summer, Roseland was ripe for some form of conflict.

This particular day the block seemed to be extra packed with people selling an escape from the ghetto in plastic bags, manila envelopes, and vials. Young thugs, little girls with big bellies, and others playing stroller wars on uneven sidewalks covered in litter seemed to be out in droves today.

Jaleesa had just gotten off the city bus to visit her old neighborhood. As soon as she stepped off the 34 South Michigan, she was approached by one of the young thugs on the street.

"Aye, aye girl!" The dusty looking kid said approaching her. Jaleesa rolled her eyes and kept walking like she hadn't heard the shit he said.

"Oh so you gone act like a bitch, huh?" The youngster said in a threatening voice.

"Who are you calling a bitch?" Jaleesa inquired. "Yo momma ain't outside today!" A few people walking down the street laughed at her comment.

"Yo, I slap bitches for disrespecting me." The dude threatened.

"And I mace and slice niggas who got the balls to run up!" Jaleesa proclaimed holding her fighters stance.

As the dude started to approach her, Jaleesa pulled out her mace ready for him to step one inch closer.

"You better get back nigga." She warned.

"Bitch you gonna learn some…"

Before the guy could finish his sentence, he was backhanded by Juicy, one of the guys from the block that Jaleesa had grown up on.

"Dude, we don't disrespect females on this block." Juicy said angrily. "Get yo little dirty ass up!" He continued, grabbing the kid roughly by the collar. "Take that bullshit back over the tracks where it belongs. Yo ass ain't even supposed to be around here little Cortez, I told you the next time I caught you I was gone beat your thieving little ass. Now get the fuck out of here!"

Cortez got up and broke so fast you would have thought Juicy had pulled a hammer out on him.

"Thanks for the rescue Juicy," Jaleesa said giving him a hug.

"No prob ma, shorty been around here stealing niggas packs for a minute. I told him when I caught him again it was a done deal. Maybe I won't see his little ass sneaking around here no more." Juicy chuckled. "So what's good with you Le Le?"

"I came over here to see what Tasha and I are getting into tonight, but by the looks of the block, I don't have to wait until tonight," Jaleesa replied.

"I thought maybe you were coming to see me." Juicy teased playfully, although if she was biting, he was definitely ready to reel her in.

Jaleesa had known him since they were in grade school at Curtis Elementary. He was one of the kids that used to get picked on because he didn't always have the newest shoes and name brand clothes. Caleb, which was Juicy's real name, was raised by a hardworking mother who couldn't afford the extras that she knew her growing sons wanted. All of her three sons answered the call of the streets in one way or another. His oldest brother was doing a short bid for armed robbery in Statesville Prison while the middle brother was fighting a federal dope case now. He was the only one of his mother's sons still on the streets, and he planned to keep it that way.

Juicy had answered the call too but tried to learn from the mistakes of his two big brothers, who were incarcerated for lengthy bids. His mother prayed for him every day that he stay out of harm's way and prison. So far, God had listened to those prayers. He sold a little weed on the side to help his mom out, but other than that, he went to school and got fairly decent grades. The advice his mom gave stuck in his head constantly, that education was the only way out of this mess. Although he didn't have a plan, he knew he was destined to be more than what he was.

"You wish Juice, there go my bitches right now," Jaleesa said seeing her friend Tasha and her acquaintance Kristen walk out of Zach's, the neighborhood liquor store.

"Le Le!" Tasha yelled out running to her best friend like she hadn't seen her in months, even though it had only been two weeks.

"Hey, sister," Jaleesa replied, greeting Tasha with a hug. "What's up Kristen?" She said acknowledging Tasha's buddy, whom she couldn't stand.

She only tolerated Kristen because she knew Tasha considered her a friend, but since Jaleesa had known her, she'd never trusted her. Unlike Kristen, Tasha and Jaleesa had known each other since the womb. Their mother's had been best friends back in the day, so it was only natural that their first born children follow the same progression. Jackie, who was Tasha's mother, and Lena, who was Jaleesa's mother, met in high school after Lena's parents bought a home in the Roseland community. Those were the days before the massive white flight, brought on by a somewhat prosperous black middle class who wanted to own their piece of the American pie.

They had met in English class. Jackie passed a note to Lena asking her was she new, and where she was from. She ended the note by asking her did she want to be her friend, concluding that pretty girls had to stick together. That elicited a laugh and a yes from Lena, and they'd been friends ever since.

The new high school was a new experience for Lena, who previously attended a private Catholic school with white students. Until recently, blacks weren't admitted to the school, but with the neighborhood's changing demographic, the administration found it necessary to accept them to keep the school running. Many whites had left the district for the suburban areas of Chicago. For the first time, she found herself having to fight because she was pretty, light-skinned, had long hair and was exceptionally smart.

Jackie was from the neighborhood and used to the jealousy. Her family, the Johnsons, had money, so she was always dressed in the latest styles and fashions and kept spending money in her pocket. Many days they went toe to toe with girls from the neighborhood who called them sellouts and wannabes. They kicked butt from Roseland to Pullman and became inseparable; you never saw one without the other. Their daughters were the same way.

"I miss you, friend," Tasha exclaimed, hugging Jaleesa one more time. "Now that y'all done moved on up, you act like you too good for the hood." Tasha joked.

"Girl please, you know I'm hood thru and thru."

"I know that's right." Interjected Kristen, slapping high fives with Jaleesa, on one of the few occasions in which the girls agreed on something. "I saw you ready to mace little Cortez thieving ass."

"I wish you would have, the little fucker snatched my purse last week. Tried to say it wasn't him cause he had on a mask, but I know those beat up ass Mikes' anywhere!" She said referring to his tennis shoes that gave up the ghost a long time ago.

The girls laughed and cracked jokes on the short walk to Tasha's building. It was a three flat on 113th Street right off Michigan Avenue, and as far as Roseland went, and it was right in the thick of things.

Tasha's family, the Johnson's, had owned this building for as long as Jaleesa could remember. Tasha's mom was raised here and Lena, Jaleesa's mom, had spent countless nights here with her friend when they were growing up. Back then, it had been three separate apartments and had remained that way until the summer of third grade for Tasha and Jaleesa.

Back then the girls were truly inseparable. If they weren't at Jackie's house, they were at Lena's parents' house down the street. To Lena and Jackie, it was as if they both had two daughters instead of one. If Lena bought Jaleesa an outfit, she had to get her baby Tasha one too. If Jackie bought Tasha a charm bracelet, she had to get her niece Jaleesa one too.

See Jackie and Lena were so close that they had even gotten pregnant around the same time. Jackie was a little more free hearted than Lena had been and was the first to lose her virginity. Jackie's boyfriend, Allen, had finally talked her into it and built up courage enough himself to go for it. Everyone knew her twin brothers Raymond and Charles would maim and kill over their little sister. So Allen had to tread lightly. It took about three sexual encounters for Jackie to get pregnant.

Being the sheisty street dealer he was, when Jackie told Allen she was knocked up, he immediately denied paternity. All that got him was a severe ass kicking from the twins, and a promise that if he ever showed his face out south again, his mother wouldn't recognize it at his funeral. Needless to say, Allen was never seen again.

Lena, on the other hand, hid her pregnancy for as long as she could. She didn't want her parents to be disappointed in her. When she found out she was pregnant, she cried for days, not wanting to disappoint her parents, and not wanting anyone to know who the father was. It wasn't because she didn't love him, or because he didn't love her, no one even knew they had messed around, and it had only been one moment of indiscretion, a secret they both vowed to take to the grave.

"It's Richard, ain't it?" Jackie questioned as she tried to guess the father of her best friend's baby. "Bitch why you being so secretive? You must not know who it is."

"You got me messed up girl," Lena said chuckling. "If I haven't answered you in the last nine years what makes you think I'm telling you now."

It had been a sore spot in the friendship, the only sore spot. When Jackie found out Lena was pregnant, she was ecstatic. They had always wanted to do everything together anyway; this would be the best. However when she inquired as to who fathered little Jaleesa, her friend was always quick to clam up and say she didn't want to discuss it.

"As long as my baby is taken care of, what should it matter," or "I'm her momma and daddy," were usually the answers to inquiries about Jaleesa's dad. It had hurt Jackie's feelings that her best friend wouldn't divulge the information. She wasn't sure if Lena was scared she was going to tell someone, or judge her. Over the years, she learned to stop asking and be grateful that she wasn't alone being a single parent, though. Her best friend was right by her side.

"So where are we going tonight?" Lena inquired.

"Girl there is a party going on at Barbra's lounge, and the Cadillac club down the hill. I say we start down the hill and make our way up." Jackie said hitting a joint she had cuffed from her brother Raymond's stash.

"Girl, when will you get enough of them crazy ass niggas from down the hill?" Lena laughed pulling the joint from Jackie's hand.

"As long as they spending money girl, it's all good. I know where my heart lays, though, right here on Michigan Ave." She said slapping palms with Lena. "Anyway bitch, are you ever going to tell me who your baby daddy is?"

****

After, dropping Jaleesa and Tasha off with Lena's parents for the night, Lena and Jackie made their way to the Cadillac Club by walking down the hill, cutting through Palmer Park. Although it might have been safer to go around, they had their trusty cans of mace and razors and weren't too worried about anything happening to them. When they got in the Cadillac, it was juking! The little lounge was filled to capacity and beyond as people tried to get a glimpse of the big players in attendance.

Jackie and Lena walked with their heads held high like they owned the club and were let in without any qualms.

"Ugghh, I hate those stank bitches." One of the neighborhood rats said as she eyed the two friends. "One day they're going to realize they ain't the shit! All they are is overpriced hoes!"

"I know right, I used to beat those bitches ass on a regular in high school." One of the other girls spoke out.

Everyone knew she was lying, seeing as how Jackie and Lena never lost a one on one fight in high school. When the jealous girls finally made it to the door, the bouncer informed them that they were at capacity.

"What?" The chubby loudmouth girl said. "We have been in line for an hour, and y'all just let them bitches walk right up in here? Y'all tripping for real."

Once Jackie and Lena got in the club, there were dudes buying drinks from every corner of the bar. The music was pumping, weed was in the air, and niggas were spending money like it was going out of style. They were kicking it until Jackie heard a familiar voice.

"What the fuck you doing down the hill?"

"Oh, shit!" Jackie jumped spilling her drink at the sound of her big brother's voice.

"Didn't I tell you to stay from down this hill? You know how these crazy niggas get down. I don't want to have to kill a nigga over my little sister." Charles stated.

"And that goes for your ass too Lena." He said giving her a stern look. "I can name at least one person who I know for a fact doesn't want you down here." He said eyeing her up and down.

"And who is that?" Jackie asked, wanting to know what she was missing.

"Just get yo shit and let's ride little sis," Charles ordered, obviously not in the mood for bullshit.

Jackie rolled her eyes and gathered her things. "My big brothers are such fucking haters sometimes! I'm a grown ass woman with a baby and still can't do shit." She said shaking her head. "God they get on my nerves."

"Go wait in the car," Charles said handing them the keys. "I'll be out in a minute. I need to see a man about a dog."

Jackie snatched the keys and proceeded to walk out the club.

"I see somebody got sent to the principal's office." The chubby girl spat. She had an awful lot of shit to talk, even though her fat ass was still waiting in line,

"I know this fat sloppy bitch ain't talking to me?" Jackie asked looking at Lena.

All Lena could think was, "Damn I haven't had a fight since high school, here we go…"

Very few words were exchanged before Jackie hauled off and muffed the chubby girl. Before you knew it, two of her sidekicks thought to jump in, but before they could, Lena stole on the one who was talking shit earlier and began to go to work. The other friend stood on the sideline afraid of getting her ass kicked.

"Here come the boys!" Someone outside the club sounded the alarm for police approaching the scene.

People began to scatter like roaches at a grape stomp. Forgetting about waiting for Charles, Jackie and Lena quickly made their way from the crime scene and fled to the park.

"Girl that shit was fun," Jackie said out of breath and trying to laugh. "We ain't whipped ass like that since high school."

"I know right, I am out of practice like a mug." Lena laughed along.

As the sounds of the sirens died, the girls started to slow their pace through the park, so as to not look suspicious. As they crossed pass the basketball courts, Lena noticed Raymond's car parked at the corner.

"Oh girl, there go Ray right there. He will give us a ride to Barbara's and hit our hands. Let's hurry up before he rolls."

As the girls sped up their walking to get to Raymond, they noticed two dudes sneaking from the alley on some creep type shit.

"I know these niggas ain't trying to rob my brother!" Jackie said furiously. "That shit ain't happening."

With that Jackie hollered her brother's name trying to catch his attention, at that moment, he looked up and was hit from behind with a gun.

Jackie, now oblivious to her friend Lena, began running in her brother's direction. It was instinct, family always comes first. The ties that bind are the ties that keep us together," is what her daddy always told them; a code they never broke. "Never let any nigga break those ties, they are all that you have." That was the only thought in her mind as she raced to save her brother.

"What are they doing out here this late?" Raymond thought right before he was knocked semi-unconscious with the stick-up kid's gun. Raymond and Charles had been out that night conducting a large business transaction. It was going to be what put them on top of the game. He was here to cop about ten keys from some cats out west who were selling straight butter. He and his twin brother had made a name for themselves out here, but they wanted their name to ring throughout the city, and this was just the move to make that happen.

His Godfather Abraham, who had been in the game since the 40's, doing everything from bootlegging to pimping, to selling drugs, put him and his brother on when they graduated high school. All was supposed to be good, but Raymond's godfather had not known about the larceny in the hearts of the mules he sent to make the drop. They figured they could make off with the drugs and the money. Never understanding how far Abraham's reach truly went, and never knowing the twins were his family. Unfortunately, the two thieves would soon find out.

"Get ready to die, nigga!" Jackie said running up behind one of the dudes, completely slicing his ear off with her razor.

He grabbed his ear in pain and fell to the ground, as Lena came up and maced the other guy, causing him to drop his weapon. Meanwhile, Jackie was in the car leaning over Raymond trying to wake him up.

"Please, big bro get up, get up!" She pleaded.

Raymond groaned in pain. Looking around to make sure the bandits had run off, Lena approached the car. Seeing all the blood made her think Raymond was dead. The sight instantly brought her to tears.

"Not Raymond, not now, not like this." She thought.

"I'm good little sis," Raymond said, holding Lena's hand. "Them niggas gonna get it!"

The sound of sirens made everyone jump out of the car and try to get moving.

"Wait a minute!" Raymond yelled. "Get that cash and product out the car, my prints all over that shit, I ain't trying to go to nobody's jail tonight. Jackie put on my coat, you should be able to fit a few bricks in the arms without looking suspicious."

Jackie slid on her big brother's warm sable half-length coat. It was a little big for her, but she could manage without dropping anything out the sleeves.

"Lena, you can fit some in that damn suitcase you call a purse." Ray joked. "I'll carry the cash, of course, you know how y'all are."

Just as they began their journey back to home base, which was three blocks away, two shots rang out and instinct dictated that they run. Lena had never run that fast in her life as she stayed determined not to run in a straight line, fearing being shot over some bullshit. Her only thought was to make it to the house. When Lena reached the Johnson's building, she didn't see Jackie or Raymond. As she went to reach for the doorbell, she was scared half to death by Charles coming through the gangway.

"What's going on," Charles said his voice pumping with adrenaline. "I got to the car, y'all was gone, and I heard shots. Where are my peeps at Lena?" Charles asked, noticing Jackie was nowhere around. Only then did Lena break down in tears and hurriedly explain what had just gone down. Before she could finish, Charles was fleeing down the hill.

"Jackie, Jackie please says something, baby." Raymond cried as he held his little sister.

She had been the one to take the bullet meant for her brother. The stick-up kid who had his ear cut off had doubled back and decided he could at least leave with the dope. When he saw the girl go down, he knew his partner was still alive and Raymond was distracted. Now was his chance.

"I'm sorry Jackie. I'm sorry little sister." Raymond said still rocking Jackie in his arms.

He turned around when he felt someone running up behind him. It was Charles, and the look on his face was enough to break his heart all over.

"Not Jax," Charles said calling Jackie by the nickname he gave her. As Charles knelt down beside his little sister, he knew what needed to be done. It was death for all who were behind this and everyone close to them. His little sister completed the trinity of Johnson greatness, and her young life had been snuffed out.

"Where them niggas at," Charles asked wiping a tear from his eye.

"I don't know man, after I saw Jackie fall..." Raymond trailed off.

"Alright, you got a burner on you?" He asked his twin. Raymond nodded his head in reply.

"Alright, brother. What I'm going to tell you is going to hurt you to your heart, but you have to do it. Leave Jax here we got to find them niggas before they get in the wind." Charles stated matter of fact.

"I can't leave my baby sister dead in the gutter."

"Ray this is war," Charles said sternly. "Ain't shit you can do behind those bars. The boys will be here in a minute, I hear the sirens. We got business to handle."

Raymond took one last look at his beautiful little sister. Closed her eyes and laid her gently on the ground.

"There those niggas go," The stick-up kid said, "crying over that little bitch."

"Shut the fuck up man, do you know who we just killed? We weren't supposed to kill any one, let alone her!" TJ spat.

He was scared as hell. When word got back to Abraham about what happened, he was a dead man. There was supposed to be no larceny involved; make the drop, bring the money back, but no, TJ decided to listen to Bucky. He wanted to run off with the dope and money and lay low at his sister crib in Iowa, but right now, Iowa wasn't far enough. They were going to have to kill the twins in order to get out of this one. To have them and Abraham after him at the same time would mean certain death.

"They haven't gone too far." Whispered Charles, following the trail of blood from Bucky's sliced off ear.

The drops stopped at the beginning of an alley, and they could hear faint voices coming from a garage. The idiots had cornered themselves. Knowing TJ and Bucky had firepower the twins decided to give them time to come out. Within a matter of minutes Bucky stepped out of the side door of the garage and was quickly silenced with a blast of Raymond's gun. Raymond paid no attention to the brain matter that now covered his hoodie and face. He wiped his mouth and went in for TJ.

"Man hold on, hold on. It wasn't supposed to be like this." TJ said trying to explain his way out of death.

"Who sent you?" Charles asked, letting TJ know then and there he wasn't surviving no matter what.

Tears began to stream down TJ's cheeks as he opened his mouth to plead one more time, but he was kicked in it by Raymond.

"Save your prayer for God, bitch ass nigga, because tonight you die!"

Angry because he felt as if Abraham had given him a death sentence; although Abraham specifically told him not to try the twins, knowing TJ'S character. It had been a test and he failed miserably.

"Abraham," was the last words TJ's sheisty ass ever uttered before Charles ushered him into death.

When the key in the door turned, Lena was too scared to ask where Jackie was, she didn't want to fear the worst. Raymond dropped the bag on the floor and sat down on the couch next to Lena.

With a heavy sigh he said, "They killed my baby sister. The coat." He stuttered. "They thought she was me because of the coat. I killed my baby sister."

Raymond repeated these words over and over as tears streamed down his face. Lena held him in her arms and let him cry. He had only done that once before; the night his father had died.

Jackie's death came as a heavy blow to the twins Charles and Raymond, as well as Lena. She felt as if as she had lost her sister and best friend in one day. The funeral service was beautiful. Raymond sat next to Lena in stoic silence, although Lena could tell his mind was working. She just hoped that whatever it was didn't cause more death. She squeezed his hand.

After Raymond had told her of Jackie's death, he and Charles took some soldiers and immediately rained down on the West side crew that had been responsible. In 48 hours, a three block radius in K-town became a war zone. No one was off limits women, children, even the elderly if they happened to catch a stray bullet. Every day until the day of Jackie's funeral, blood filled the gutters, and K-town almost looked abandon after the twins had given orders to kill anything moving on the streets.

Looking at Raymond made Lena have nervous butterflies in her stomach, for more reasons than the obvious. She knew what he was capable of, but she had never seen it firsthand, just stories Jackie used to tell her. To be honest, she always thought Jackie was exaggerating, but now she knew every story she'd told was the truth. The way the colors from the stained glass windows danced off of Raymond's face, he almost looked like an angel in deep thought. However Lena knew, not one of those thoughts came from on high.

A few months after Jackie's death many changes occurred. Lena moved out of the neighborhood with the help of the twins, Raymond specifically. She no longer wanted to live in the neighborhood where her childhood best friend and innocence had been stolen over a dope man's dream. Jackie's death helped open her eyes to the fact that all the streets offered were a fast life and even faster death. She decided to start nursing school and had never looked back. She didn't want to raise Jaleesa in the neighborhood. It just wasn't the same anymore.

The twins had eventually come to a peace agreement with Abraham. There had been much bloodshed on both sides, so an agreement was made. The twins would control the Southside, from Roseland to the Altged Gardens, and Abraham would control the Westside as always. The three men shook hands and went their separate ways. Since that day there had never beef between the Johnson family and Abraham. If a situation arose, it was quickly resolved and the parties resumed their business as usual. Eventually the twins were able to control an empire that reached beyond drugs and illegal activities.

After the fallout of Jackie's death, it was rumored that Abraham gave up the game completely to pursue a career in city politics. He fared very well actually. He had been alderman of one of the west side wards for over thirteen years now and was prosperous due to other businesses to. However, in this world peace rarely last forever, and the new generation of thugs rarely respected the game and were making a mockery of it. Over the years both the twins and Abrahams power and wealth grew, while the quality, integrity, and loyalty of what it meant to be a boss deteriorated.

CHAPTER 2

Daughters

"So what's cracking for the night?" Kristen said, opening a freezing cold bottle of Remy they had just copped from Zach's.

"I say we hit up Rainbow Beach this evening ladies, or the Bungalows, they usually have a few ballers out and about this time of year." Tasha replied, sipping on a mix of Remy and apple juice.

Rainbow Beach and the Bungalows were popular hangout spots on Lake Michigan that were often frequented by the urban population of Chicago. During the summertime, you would be guaranteed to find the beach full of young people, and a few old timers too, drinking, smoking, playing music and trying to get into something for the night. Some nights it was so popping on the beach people figured why pay to get into a club, when all the meat was on the street. Tonight would be no exception for the girls.

"Man, y'all ain't said shit about no beach!" Jaleesa griped. "I ain't bring no beach clothes, I bought club clothes. I can't wear this Baby Phat dress and heels on nobody's beach!"

"Calm down. You know Mama T only rocks the hottest shit in the hood and you are lucky because we wear the same size, just about." Tasha joked.

"I know my ass is bigger than yours." Jaleesa joked.

"You ain't offer me anything to wear to the beach." Kristen whined, feeling left out like she always did when Jaleesa came around.

"Oh stop pouting Kristen, you just brought a new DKNY swimsuit last week you ain't even rocked yet. Why you all in my closet?" Tasha said playfully.

"Man, you always act funny when Jaleesa come around here. Its sister this, and sister that, but when she ain't here you all in my ass." Kristen spat, offended.

"Never will I ever be in any ass but my own, and that's only when I'm pulling my draws out of it!" Tasha quipped.

"Hey don't put me in your love triangle." Jaleesa tried to joke to break the tension in the room.

Although she never liked Kristen, she wanted tonight to go as smoothly as possible and didn't want to have to get in that bitch ass. Jaleesa had to admit that although Tasha lived, breathed, and ate hood, she never dressed like it. While all the other girls were rocking Baby Phat, Akademik, and Aeropostle, she came with Donna Karen, Michael Kors, and Vivienne Tann; names most of these ghetto girls had never heard of or could even pronounce. To be honest, she put Kristen and Jaleesa on the hottest designers, and usually gave them what she didn't want. She was always a step ahead with the latest fashions, and the hood rats were constantly trying to imitate, but they couldn't even compare.

"Chill, chill Ladies." Tasha said passing the bottle. "Let's hop in Kristen's car and go to Oakbrook Mall. I'll get both you bitches something to wear. Lord knows I can't be seen with some bum ass bitches." She laughed out loud.

"Whatever," Kristen said grabbing her car keys. "And why we got to go all the way to Oakbrook?" Kristen complained. "The plaza is right on 95th."

Tasha and Jaleesa gave each other a look that said it all.

"Bitch, why are you so low budget?" Tasha blurted out, with Jaleesa laughing on the side. "Someone wants to take you to Red Lobster and you ask for Mc Donald's? Kristen my friend, you have a lot to learn." Tasha said placing her arm around Kristen shoulder. "You need to get ya game up, love."

"What? It's a lot closer than Oakbrook, I'm just saying." Kristen didn't understand what was wrong with wanting to shop at the Plaza, all the neighborhood girls that had a little dough got their gear from there.

These bourgeoisie bitches always think they better than me, Kristen thought to herself. *I'm gonna show they ass sooner, rather than later.*

Every hood, ghetto, project, HUD housing complex, or whatever you call it, had a chick like Kristen. Hell, they were millions of chicks like Kristen, jealous hearted. She was the type of person who spoke of friendship, but didn't truly know what it was to be a friend. It was in her nature to be envious of anything someone else had that she didn't.

Kristen had met Tasha shortly after Jaleesa moved off the block. The girls were just entering the fourth grade and Tasha was really missing Jaleesa, when Kristen's family moved across the street from the Johnson's building. Kristen was a quiet little girl, who was picked on because her mother, Caroline, was a crack head and didn't know who her father was. Kristen's saving grace was that she had an older sister, Samantha, who was able to hustle, to keep her little sister feed, and clean, if not properly clothed.

Once the two girls became friends, Kristen never wanted to leave Tasha's side. Tasha knowing she was across the street hungry most of the time made sure when Kristen came over she was feed, and always left with an outfit, some shoes, and anything else to help her out in the wardrobe department. Tasha felt bad for her friend, and in the sixth grade when she told her Uncle Charles where all her new clothes and toys were going. He took pity on the little girl and her sister Samantha, who was selling nickel bags just to support herself and her sister. From that day forward, Tasha never had to give Kristen food or clothes.

You would think that Kristen and Samantha would forever be grateful to the Johnson family. Samantha was, but Kristen was only when she was with Tasha. After a while her gratefulness for all that had been done for her turned into envy for what Tasha had. Kristen said thank you for the clothes Tasha gave her, but something in her wanted to scream. Since they'd entered their teens, it had only gotten worse. It seemed like Kristen was always in competition with Tasha, especially when Jaleesa was around. She once asked Tasha why she never called her sister, to which Tasha replied that she and Jaleesa had a special bond that no one can break. After Tasha saw the hurt look in Kristen's eyes she added,

"Oh Krissy, don't be like that you my favorite roadie. Ride till we die right?"

"Yeah, until we die." Kristen answered, but the damage had been done.

Kristen hated Jaleesa. It was because of her Tasha would never see her as a sister, an equal. She would always see her as the dirty little girl across the street the Johnson family saved.

Kristen's car was an old beater. A 2001 Ford Taurus that had seen better days, yet Kristen tried to treat it like it was a fully loaded 2011 May Bach.

"Stop dumping ashes on my floor Jaleesa!" Kristen snapped peering at her through the rearview mirror.

"Well what do you want me to do, the raggedy ass window doesn't roll down! Dump ashes in my hand?" Jaleesa retorted.

"Use the cup. Tasha stop laughing and hand that bitch the cup." She said with a little too much venom.

"First off Kristen, I'm not your bitch, second of all, this trap is not the royal carriage. It already has cigarette burns in the back seats!" Jaleesa spat back.

"Well, you can get back on your carriage, you call the CTA!"

"Chill y'all." Tasha said after she ceased her laughing fit. "Y'all are always fighting like cats and dogs. Let's get to where we going first."

"Forget this raggedy mug." Jaleesa mumbled under her breath.

She remembered the day Kristen had driven on the block in that trap six months ago. Her story was that some low budget baller had bought her the car. The real story however was he brought the car for himself in her name, since he didn't have a valid license, and ended up getting a long bid. She went and took the car from his momma's house in the dead of night. Guess she didn't want his sisters to get in that ass. They couldn't report the car stolen because no one had a title so it was basically a grab-n-go car.

She thought she was the shit pulling up in front of Tasha's house. Tasha had pumped her up like she really did something and all Jaleesa could do was look and shake her head. Kristen implied Jaleesa was a hater.

"If all your pussy is worth is a beater of a car, then you need to tighten up!" Jaleesa said.

Kristen was so mad everyone that was out that day had a good laugh at her expense. She felt like a dirty little girl all over again. Tasha saw the look in Kristen's eyes and stepped in between the two before they got to fighting.

Although they were both her friends, there was not a doubt whose side she would be riding out on that day, the ties bind always. She didn't want to let it get there.

"Le Le, you bogus than a mofo. Really girl? Our friend made a come up today and you hating on her."

Because the girls new each other so well, Jaleesa knew she had put Tasha in a bad predicament. When she went home Tasha really only had Kristen as a friend. She knew Kristen didn't like her, and she didn't care for her either; she squashed it for Tasha's sake.

"Well let's stop talking and go on 43rd to cop some gristle in Krissy's new car." Jaleesa said forcing a smile. "Let's put the wheels to good use."

After the girls had spent themselves out at Oakbrook, Tasha treated them to lunch at Ruth's Chris Steak House. When Kristen asked for hot sauce, and continued to run their waiter back and forth for this or that, Tasha began to have second thoughts about bringing Kristen here.

"Girl as much as this steak cost up in here, we need our money's worth." Kristen shot, a little too loudly, causing other diners to take notice.

When they finally got the check Kristen blurted out again, "Damn Tasha, this shit is like $250 for lunch? How can I be down?"

If Tasha didn't catch the tone, Jaleesa sure did and decided to watch Kristen closely. A jealous female will do whatever it takes to get what you got.

"Okay chicks, let's roll up out of here. It's getting late and I need a nap before we go to this beach tonight. I'm going to ask my Uncle Charles can I get one of his whips tonight so we can ride in style. No offense Krissy." She said quickly, knowing how sensitive the girl was about her car. "Remember ladies, money attracts money. The more we appear to have, the more they spend."

"Good, I'm tired of all these white folks. Let's get back to the hundreds where all the color is." Kristen laughed, causing Jaleesa to think about how ghetto this chick really was.

CHAPTER 3

Sharks at the Beach

After much begging, pleading, and finally compromising, Charles gave in and let Tasha take his brand new, barley driven 2010 Acura out for the night.

"The rules are, no smoking, drinking, or dudes in my whip niece."

He tried to sound stern, but Tasha knew he was soft as putty. The only reason it took her so long to finagle this ride was because it was not her first choice, or second for that matter. She had originally asked for the plum purple Porsche he had let her drive a few times on Lakeshore Drive and down town. Finding out she would be going to Rainbow Beach in his whip definitely made the answer a no. She tried for the Range Rover and lost, because he had some product in there. She settled for the Acura. It was hot, but she wanted to stunt hard. Anyone who knew anything about the game in Chicago knew her uncles, which in essence meant they knew her. She'd waited until her eighteenth birthday to shine, and the twins had thrown her a luau on the block. Free food, music, drinks and weed brought everyone in the hood out. She was destined to be a hood princess, it was in her genes. She was destined to take her mother's place on the Johnson family throne.

Since her mother's untimely death, Tasha had been showered with love, affection and whatever her heart desired from her uncles. Tasha's mother had left a nice insurance policy, but she never had to touch a dime. She never wanted for anything, so when she measured the young boys her age she found them wanting. None could compete with what her uncles provided, and they had schooled her to the game so she didn't believe anything a nigga said. Unless he was about action, she wasn't hearing it.

The guilt and anger that overcame the brothers because of their little sister's death manifested itself into street success. After the treaty with Abraham, the twins began to gain capital, which they funneled into the Roseland community. Everyone from the G (Altged Gardens) to 95th and Michigan paid homage to the twins, whether they knew it or not. Whether you were buying dope, weed, loose squares, or bootleg CD's in the land, the twins were paid from it. They owned Laundromats, beauty supply stores, nail shops and leased store fronts to business owners who sold everything from $1 tee-shirts and socks, to furniture.

Roseland was quietly owned and controlled by the twins. They literally owned the turf their people worked on. The barber shops, liquor stores, clothing stores, and everything shops, shops that had everything in supply. They sold bootleg movies, bootleg Nike's, airbrush tees, loose squares, and even weed. The twins supplied the workers with everything from illegal product, to retail goods, even security in some stores. They didn't own all of Michigan Ave, but they owned enough to keep their ears and eyes toward the streets.

"Oh, Uncle Charles I need a few dollars too." Tasha said holding her hand out.

Charles shook his head as he dug in his pocket and could only wonder where the $1500 he gave her yesterday went.

"Didn't I just give you some money the other day?"

"Yes, but that was the other day, and don't be cheap now." She said as she saw him trying to only give her $500.

Charles went to speak, but his niece's mischievous smile melted his heart. She looked just like Jax when she smiled like that. It was moments like this when his sister's spirit spoke to him the loudest.

"Alright $600, cause I know you gonna hit Raymond up." He said chuckling.

"And you know this man." She said playfully grabbing the keys and leaving out the room.

"Okay ladies, let's hit the beach." Tasha said applying lip gloss in the Acura's rearview mirror.

The girls looked nice, even Kristen, in a silk Donna Karen shirt that hung off her right shoulder paired with a pair of black BeBe jeans that looked poured on.

She obviously let Tasha put her on some make-up, Jaleesa thought. Kristen's knowledge of make-up was elementary at best. She stuck to the ghetto girl code of lip gloss and black eye liner, which was also used for lip liner. *Lord she need to step her game up*, Jaleesa thought.

The Bungalows, proved to be packed that night. You would have thought it was the first hot day of the summer seeing all the people outside. Some people had been out there all day, smoking grills, and empty liquor bottles overfilling the trash cans were telling signs.

"Man we should have come out earlier." Tasha stated, looking for somewhere to park the whip safely.

She didn't want to hear Uncle Charles' mouth if the car wasn't returned in pristine condition. Tasha swerved into a spot and received a horn and a middle finger. The girl in the other car was talking shit with the windows rolled up.

"Bitch you can get it too!" Kristen screamed out the back window to the other driver's ghetto friend who had gotten out of the car.

"Roll up my damn window! I'm too cute to fight tonight." Tasha said angrily. "Leave them broke bitches be. I bet when we get out this car they ain't gonna say shit!"

By the time Tasha finished parking, the girls had rode off in a flurry of cuss words.

"See, just like I told you." Tasha said.

"Okay we're parked, now let's roll up the dro and smoke." Jaleesa said.

"Alright hand me the sack." Kristen said.

Each girl looked at each other and came to the realization nobody had any green.

"Man why y'all didn't say neither of you were holding? We could have hit 43rd before we came out here! I ain't losing my spot." Tasha said, folding her arms like the spoiled brat she was.

"Well pop the drink I know we got that at least." Kristen said.

The girls got out of the car as Tasha popped the trunk to get the drink. After pouring cups, the girls posted up on the car to check out the action. There were a few cats strolling through there stunting like they were ballers. They were even in nice cars, but Tasha and Jaleesa were looking for the drivers of those cars not the passengers.

"Man y'all smell that? Somebody smoking some good ass weed right now." Jaleesa said.

She could find the blunt in a crowded room in record time. She was definitely the weed head of the trio. "Maybe somebody will sell us some of that shit. Let's get to mingling."

The girls refilled their cups and proceeded to follow Jaleesa's nose to the ganja. She suddenly stopped.

"Somewhere in that vicinity." She said pointing to a group of guys who looked like they belonged to a motorcycle club. "Someone over there smoking good."

"Well what are we waiting for?" Kristen asked, making her way to the crowd of motorcycle riders. She went directly to the first ember she saw light up the night. "What's good?" She asked to no one in particular. "Who got those loud packs?"

"Who wants to know?" A tall, brown-skinned dude rocking dreads asked her.

"Goddamn he is a dub!" Tasha said to Jaleesa. "He even smells like money. That is Clive Christian C cologne. That shit goes for like $400 an ounce." She informed the girls.

Jaleesa and Kristen gave her an odd look.

"What?" Tasha asked. "Jaleesa isn't the only one with a nose for green. The kind I sniff out may not be smokeable, but it sure is spendable." She said laughing.

"Amen to that." Jaleesa agreed slapping Tasha a high five.

"So, what's all the high fiving about?" The guy with the dreads asked the girls. As he sat perched atop of his brand new BMW 1600GT. "I heard someone asking where you could get some of this kill from."

"I was asking." Tasha said speaking up.

This dude looked like he was about his money. From his bike, to his Perry Ellis khaki shorts and Polo top, to his Feragamo loafers, he screamed baller without ever opening his mouth. She could tell this was her kind of guy. His dreads were freshly done, with a fresh line up. His hands were manicured with impeccably clean nails, and his teeth were a natural bright white. Damn, he was fine.

"So what's up?" Tasha inquired putting on her prettiest flirty smile. "Me and my girls was about to blow back when we realised, we were out of that good shit, and no offense, but that shit you smoking so loud, its disrespectful."

The brown skinned stranger had to laugh at that. "Oh you got jokes huh? I like that ma. There is nothing better than a feisty woman."

"So what's your name anyway?" The stranger inquired.

"Tasha and yours?"

"Mako."

"Like the shark?" Jaleesa cut in.

"Yeah like the shark."

"I thought Lake Michigan didn't have any sharks." Tasha flirted.

Mako liked this girl. Not only was she pretty, she had a personality, and sense of humour to boot. He didn't find that in the females he knew. Most of them were chicken heads with aspirations of being his, or some other hood ballers baby momma. He could sense she was different. The understated expensive clothes she wore said a lot. Whoever was taking care of her had to have some long bread. She was definitely not a gym shoe rat.

"I'm a land shark baby. I don't like fish."

"Anyway," Kristen interrupted, "can I get my smoke on while y'all get your cake on?"

"Oh I see all y'all got jokes huh?" Mako said chuckling. "Timmo let me holler at ya for a minute bro." Mako said gesturing toward a light skinned stocky dude who was dressed in a hot Akademik short outfit and some fresh white Air Force One's.

Timmo got off the seat of his Honda CB 1000R and made his way to the group.

"This is my man Tim." Mako said introducing him to the girls. "Man you still got some green on you. They were trying to blow back."

"Naw man, we smoking the last of it now, y'all can hit this if you want to." Timmo said offering the blunt to Kristen who was next in natural rotation.

When she went to reach for it, Jaleesa cut in. "Thanks and all but we don't smoke shit we ain't seen rolled."

This thirsty bitch, will smoke anything, Jaleesa thought. Rule number one of weed smoking, don't smoke what you haven't seen rolled; better yet bring your own shit to the table. Nowadays people were lacing their weed with all kind of crazy shit.

"Naw baby, we ain't on that shit. I smoke nothing but the finest." Timmo said, not the least bit offended.

He could tell that out of the three, Kristen was the hood rat. She had a nice face and a banging body that highlighted perky breast, a flat stomach, and a great ass, but he knew she was all body and no brains. Bitches like that came a dime a dozen, but the short light skinned one who had refused the blunt, he could work with that.

"I didn't get your name ma." Timmo said to Jaleesa.

"I know because I didn't give it." Jaleesa said playing hard to get.

Timmo was cute, but not her type, she did not like light-skinned dudes, let alone short ones. With heels on, she would almost be eye to eye with him and she was only five feet, four inches.

"It's like that?"

"Just about." Jaleesa said.

Mako and Tasha were exchanging information, while Jaleesa was going tit for tat with this Timmo dude. Kristen started to feel left out.

"Where the rest of ya friends at?" She inquired "This shit is for the birds, no weed, the drink almost gone, and no meat in sight." She said looking at the dwindling group of motorcycle club members. It was getting late and the police would be coming soon to clear the beach out.

"Okay so get up with me soon shorty." Mako said to Tasha. "Ya friend over there look like she is ready to bounce."

"I'll get at you tomorrow." Tasha said heading to her car.

"Damn, Mako is exactly the type of dude I been looking for." Tasha told Jaleesa and Kristen on the ride home.

Kristen sat in the back rolling her eyes. *Why is this bitch always getting the dudes with the real dough*, Kristen thought sitting in the back of the Acura. *The dude Timmo was cute and had cash too, and Jaleesa acted like her stank ass couldn't give him the time of day. I can't stand these stuck up bitches. And then they didn't even try to hook me up. That's alright every bitch has her day*, Kristen thought smiling.

"What you back there smiling about?" Jaleesa asked, peering through the passenger side visor mirror.

"Damn a chick can't smile?" Kristen said defensively.

"Why you mad, I was just asking why you so happy. Damn!"

Jaleesa knew the smile she saw on Kristen's face wasn't from happiness, it had been more of a jealous smirk. She often caught Kristen out of the corner of her eye with a look of jealousy toward Tasha and herself. She knew the girl was jealous, but Tasha tried to overlook it or just didn't see it. Jaleesa hoped she found out before Kristen crossed her friend and she had to whoop that ass.

CHAPTER 4

Sons

Mako woke up to his phone vibrating on his night stand. As he went to roll over, the movement was encumbered by a body in his way. He had no idea who the person was, just that it was a female. He could barely remember last night. After him and Timmo had left the beach, the rode down out west and went to a lounge party one of their boys was having for his birthday. Mako remembered drinking and smoking until he passed out, with some stripper grinding her ass on his dick. He could just about be sure this was her in his bed. Snoring like a stuck hog. Shaking her awake and giving her a few dollars plus cab fare home, Mako looked at his phone. It was a missed call from his grandfather.

Pops, as he called him, had been Mako's father since Mako's father was killed in a suspicious drug deal gone bad. Macon Abraham Clark Sr., Mako's father, had been a heavy player in Chicago's drug game in the late 70's thru the mid 80's. He supplied a large section of Chicago's Westside with heroin and cocaine until the obsession with crack started in the 80's. Because his cocaine connect had always supplied him with the purest, uncut form of the drug to hit the streets, the butter his product produced always sold like hot cakes.

Mako looked at the screensaver on his phone, it was a picture of his parents back when they were young. His mother's smile was the focal point of the picture. Her pretty black face, framed by a soft cascade of curls, was only enhanced by her dazzling smile. He missed his parents, especially his father, who were taken from him too soon. Pops had more than made up for the loss of his father, Macon Sr., but he could never replace him. Although Mako's grandfather had kept Macon Jr. out of the streets as much as possible, it was in his blood. When he heard the stories about his father's legacy, he knew that was his destiny to fulfil, and planned on it by any means necessary.

Mako played the role of respectful, dutiful grandson in the presence of his grandfather and his crooked political friends. It was expected, and Abraham would tolerate nothing less. As Mako tried to close his eyes and go to sleep, his mind drifted to the day when he decided he wanted to become like his father.

Macon Jr. had been sitting in the principal's office waiting for his Uncle Terry to pick him up. It was the second time this month he had been in trouble. It was his freshman year at Whitney Young High School, not even half way into the year and he had been label already. The first incident had been a fight in the locker room. Some dumb ass kid had mistaken Macon's intelligence, and quiet observation as a weakness. He decided to pick a fight, and Macon swiftly broke the bigger kids jaw. His grandfather was not available, he was always in a meeting, so Terry came to bail him out. When Macon Jr. told him what happened, Terry chuckled and told him the kid had it coming. Then he explained how Macon needed to be on his best behaviour to protect his grandfather's image.

"Only good press kid." Terry tried to reinforce.

This time it was different. Mako had been caught with a quarter pound of weed in his locker. The principal, knowing the power Macon's grandfather had within city politics, decided to reach out to him before he called the police. Principal Jackson didn't know how far his tentacles of power reached, and he didn't want to lose his position at one of the finest, award winning public schools in Chicago. Good paying jobs in the field of education were hard to find and he was not quick to let that slip away.

"Mr. Clark," the principal addressed him, "your uncle is on his way here so that we can quickly and quietly resolve this matter. I can't help but be a little perplexed, excuse me, confused as to why you have been selling drugs on school property."

Mako continued to stare absently out the window, wishing Terry would hurry up and end this lecture that he felt coming.

"Most students here don't have many parents that hold the weight your grandfather's title carries. And someone s always looking for a way to get him out of the position he has worked so hard to earn."

Mako had heard so many versions of this speech he wanted to tell dude to shut the hell up! He already knew.

"So Mr. Clark are you going to tell me where you got the marijuana? Was it from another student?"

Mako knew what was up. The principal was looking for another kid to pin the crime on. Too many staff and faculty, including school security officers had seen what had happened during fifth period. Mr Jackson was worried that his livelihood was in jeopardy. The best way to remedy the problem was to put it on the kid who had supplied Mako with the drugs; however that was information Mako wasn't willing to give.

"Mr Jackson." The intercom on his desk rang. "Mr Clark's uncle and Sergeant Dunn are here. Should I send them in?"

"Go right ahead. Ms Belle."

Mr. Jackson thought it odd that Sergeant Dunn was present, he had yet to inform him of the situation that was happening, but his curiosity welcomed him in.

After the gentlemen exchanged pleasantries, they got right down to business, Terry was the first to speak.

"First off Mr. Jackson, I would once again like to apologize on behalf of my colleague Alderman Clark. He is in a very important budget meeting and could not be disturbed. However, that should not take away from the importance of this matter" Terry said, as his eyes bore into Mako making him highly uncomfortable.

"I brought Sergeant Dunn in with me so the problem can be handled quickly and quietly if at all possible." Terry said.

Reaching into his pocket, he laid a large manila envelope on the desk of the principal. Although Mako had no clue what was in it, he knew whatever it was would get him out of this jam.

That's what I'm talking about Uncle T, he thought. "Lay down the law. Macon instigated from his mind. The envelope made Mr Jackson very nervous. He wasn't sure if it was a set up or a payoff, and why had Terry brought the police with him?

"What exactly is it that you're asking me to do?" Mr. Jackson said unsure of what else to say or do.

That is when Sergeant Dunn stepped in.

"Principal Jackson, on behalf of the Chicago police, I would like to thank you for giving us information that will help lead to the arrest of those involved in a public school related drug epidemic." He continued, pushing the envelope toward the principal, "As a token of the city's appreciation here is a small reward for your information."

Talk about some gangsta shit, Macon thought. Just wait until I'm old enough to get in those streets.

After hands were shook and the gentleman went their separate ways, Mako could barely contain himself.

"Man Uncle Terry, I didn't know you had that much pull." Mako said in wonder. "I knew you were the boss on the streets, but in the school system too? Man Uncle, you got mad gangsta, I can't wait to be like you."

Terry pulled the car over with so much ferocity Mako thought he was trying to avoid an accident. "Uncle T, what ya do that for?" Mako asked, rubbing the side of his head that had hit the passenger window when Terry swerved to the curb.

Terry was furious with Mako, he could have slapped the shit out of his nephew had he not feared Abraham's wrath. Terry had to take a few deep breaths to control his temper, he didn't want to scare his nephew, just school him to the game; a game that he had every opportunity not to play.

"Listen nephew, the choices we make today often dictate how we live the rest of our lives." Trying to find the right words to say he continued, "Before you were born, I made a choice, a choice in which I chose my friend's freedom over my own. Although I eventually beat the case, the choice I made that night decided the fate that I would live and die a gangsta. Even if I had wanted to turn back I couldn't have."

This was difficult for Terry. So many times he wondered how his life would have turned out had he not taken the rap for Macon Sr. Maybe he could have gone to college, or picked up a trade, even run for public office. Instead, he chose the life of an enforcer, a baller, a gangster, America's number one enemy, a black man with power in high places; look how much they hated President Obama. He had found his political bearings in the city on Chicago's Southside.

"What you mean T?" Macon asked confused. "Quality of life? Man your life sure looks quality to me and you never went to college a day in your life and you're successful."

"Success is in the eye of the beholder. Yeah, I got money, cars, jewellery, I can buy anything my heart desires, and I'm a hood legend, but what does that all mean? I can't share my success with a decent hard working woman, because she will shun how I get down, and all the hood rats want is my money. The life of a gangsta is one without love or loyalty. You deserve much more than that."

Mako picked up his phone and called his grandfather's office. When he couldn't reach him there he tried his cell and was sent to voicemail. He left a quick message and hopped in the shower. As the water ran and began to steam up the shower, his thoughts drifted to his father and the man he was. Mako had always thought his father was an upstanding, square citizen, but the night he overheard Terry and his grandfather speaking, about his father's past, where the root of the Clark family fortune derived from, shed light on the man Mako's father had truly been. It was a light that shined brighter than the hard working square image his grandfather always portrayed his father to be. That night Mako was indirectly introduced to the man his father truly was for the first time.

****

Mako's father, Macon Sr. had always, been business minded and ruthless when it came to the drug game. He held love for nothing and no one, until Denise came into his life. He met her downtown, he was coming from bailing one of his workers out, and she was leaving from her job at the Daily building. When he saw her with her long black hair, even blacker skin, and liquid pools of copper she had for eyes, he was in lust. When he approached her to ask her name, she had ignored him. When he asked her what her name was again, she turned around to tell him to back off, but the expensive suit, bright smile and eyes made her extend her name and eventually her phone number.

On their first date, Denise asked Macon what he did for a living. She assumed because of the way he dressed and his mannerisms he had to be a professional that worked in the downtown area. He told her he worked at the stock exchange handling commodities and finance. She really had no idea what commodities were, being as how she was an underpaid legal secretary in a Jewish law firm downtown, but it was good enough for her. Eventually he started to shower her with gifts and convinced her to quit her job that he would take care of her, and take care of her he did.

Macon leased them an apartment in the Hyde Park neighbourhood of Chicago. It was a stunning three bedroom on the second floor of a three flat apartment building. Denise was given everything her heart dreamed and desired, but what she truly desired was for Macon to keep regular business hours.

After about six months of living with Macon, Denise started to realize that with the company and hours Macon kept, coupled with the large amounts of money he spent on her and him, exactly what kind of commodity he was into. Unfortunately, it was one of the only commodities a black man from the ghetto could easily get his hands on, a commodity that offered two paths; jail or death.

It was a Friday night and Macon had planned to take Denise to her favourite restaurant, Beef and Brandy, located on State Street in Chicago's downtown. This was where it had all begun. She had insisted that their first date be a lunch date so that he wouldn't get the wrong impression. Over Denise's lunch hour, they had clicked, and found they had many things in common, so much that he begged her to ditch work that day, vowing to pay her for her time. She laughed it off as he walked her to the door of her office building. This was the place their relationship began, and this is a place he decided to start a new chapter. That night Macon was going to propose to this woman that he had come to not only love and care for, but respect, and respect from him was hard to come by.

"Hey baby love." Macon said calling Denise from his car phone. "I got a few runs to make before I pick you up for dinner. Be ready by eight, and wear that red dress I brought you last week."

"Alright love, but what time is our reservations for? We need to talk when you get here." Denise said.

Macon knew what talk meant to Denise. It meant she had a bone to pick with him, and unless they came to a compromise, they wouldn't be going to dinner tonight.

"Uh oh. That doesn't sound too promising." Macon joked a bit nervously.

"Just make sure you make it here in enough time." Denise said. "My mouth is watering for a steak from Beef and Brandy right about now."

"Alright Niecy." Macon said, calling her by the pet name he had for her.

He thought it would soften the blow to whatever conversation she had in mind for him. He could only wonder what she wanted to talk about. He loved her with all his heart, but he had strayed a few times. He was very careful though, always using protection, and never sleeping with the same woman more than twice. He had made that mistake once before and almost had to kill a chick because she caught feelings and threatened to wreck his happy home. It had him wondering would she accept the ring.

Denise paced the floor of their en suite bathroom. She had just taken a second pregnancy test in the last hour to see if the result still said positive. She had been very careful in taking her birth control pills every day, but last month she caught a viral infection and unbeknownst to her, made her form of contraception null and void.

"I can't believe this." She said aloud. "I do not want a kid right now, and I don't think Macon does either."

Macon did not want children, he expressed it on many occasions in the three years they had been together. He had always used a condom up until recently. When he trusted her enough to believe that she took birth control faithfully every day, and was not sleeping with other men he allowed himself the honour and pleasure of exploring her body without barriers. That night he made a commitment to her subconsciously that he was in it for the long run. This was the second time in his life in which he slept with a woman unprotected. The first time didn't turn out this well, but the first woman was not Denise, couldn't even compare. This was his wife with or with a ring.

"What if he thinks I trapped him? He might kick me out and then where would I go?" She continued talking to herself.

As she looked around at the apartment and all the luxurious things in it, she realized he had paid for it all, even the underwear she had on.

"Damn, they always say women trap men with babies, but it looks like they have really trapped themselves."

If Macon didn't take well to her being pregnant, things could go completely downhill from there. Another thing that was bothering Denise was that she'd found a hidden compartment crafted out of the hardwood floors in the back of the closet. Although they had lived there for three years, she never happened to come to this part of the walk in. It was stacks and stacks of boxes of shoes that's she had worn once or twice, some she had to admit she didn't even remember wearing, but in trying to compose the perfect outfit for this evening, to break the news to Macon, she had purged her closet for the right outfit, shoes, and accessories.

She didn't even notice it until she went to pile the boxes back up and noticed the slightly uneven floor. She only noticed it because she had doubts about the questionable looking characters Macon had employed to refinish the hardwood floors throughout the apartment last year. As she knelt down for closer inspection, she noticed a small gap in some of the planks, just large enough to grasp the edges to open it, but virtually undetectable.

A wave of nausea swept through Denise's belly as she remembered a saying her grandmother had.

"Don't ask a question, if you can't handle the answer."

It was her way of saying, don't open Pandora's Box, but she couldn't help lifting the hatch on the hidden door not knowing what she would find, she asked the question. The answer was a safe, a safe with an electronic numerical key that she was sure only Macon knew the combination too. There were a million things that could be in that safe and she was sure whatever it was would answer the question as to how he truly made his money.

Macon looked at the clock, he had to get going, it was almost 5:30 and he had spent most of his day clearing up loose ends. When he decided to propose to Denise, he had also decided to give up the game and go legit. Although Macon was making money in the streets, he could have made a healthy amount going legit also. His father Abraham had turned his profitable street hustles into legitimate business throughout the city. This gave him not only a way to cover up his illegitimate gains, but a way to begin to fund political successes Abraham saw in his near future. He knew politics, greed, and power ruled the city government that had always been full of crooks.

Many don't know, but that is how Chicago got its nickname the Windy City. Not for the strong winds that often pervade the city no matter what season, but for the long winded officials and politicians that could talk your ear off to gain a vote. Not much had changed, they stilled talked like all other politicians, but had created a corrupt network that had a history based on stuffing ballot boxes and paying for votes. Even people who worked for the city had some part in it. Most got their jobs because they knew someone else who worked for the city and got it. Those were decent paying jobs, with good benefits, and Abraham decided blacks needed a piece of the pie too.

Abraham had told Macon he had proven himself in the streets, now it was time to take that college education and play a big boys game. He was ready. He was on his way to his last stop before home. He was about to give his right hand man Terry the keys to his kingdom. Terry was hungry for the paper, loved the fast life, fast women and the money that came with it too. Since they had met in the alley shooting dice as teens they were thick as thieves. Macon had put Terry up on the dope game once he knew he could be trusted, and they had been getting money together ever since. Terry had always been loyal to Macon, and Macon knew that he would continue to remain loyal to the Clark family's street ties.

Equally, Terry was ready to prove himself worthy to his best friend, as well as the game. The Clark family had taken Terry in as a teen and Abraham had been like a surrogate father to him, often treating him as if he were one of his own sons. Terry had proved his loyalty to the Clark family by taking a petty possession charge for Macon. Before the police could realize who Macon's father was, Terry had already copped to the half an ounce of weed under the driver's seat.

Terry had never been to jail before until that point. He had no idea what he would encounter. He was thrown into a large holding cell that was overcrowded with all levels of criminals. Rapist, murders, con artist, and petty dope dealers were yelling loudly for a CO to remove some hype who looked like he was overdosing right there. By the time a CO finally arrived the man's body was laying prostrate in a pool of his bodily waste. He looked dead to Terry, and although he did not want to look he couldn't help but to stare and wonder why no one was coming to help.

"Walker. Terrance Walker!" A CO hollered out. "Somebody just posted your bail. Now you got thirty n seconds to make it to the bars or wait for the next call." The red pocked faced guard said.

Terry made it to the bars before the guard did, he was so ready to get out of there. I knew Macon would come through, he thought.

However, it was not Macon that came to bail him out, it was Abraham who waited in the black Lincoln as he walked out of the police station. He was surprised to see him there.

"Mr. Clark, let me explain..." Terry began.

"There is nothing to explain son. What you did was not only stupid, but honourable. You just showed that you would lay down your life for my son. You should never hold another man's life in higher esteem than your own." He schooled the young boy.

"I'm sorry." Terry mumbled under his breath.

"Don't be sorry, be careful son." Abraham said.

From that day forward, Terry was on the road to street success. Abraham had been wondering who would handle the small business ventures he had Macon taking care of before he went to college. Now Terry could help ensure that his flow of drug money from Chicago's west side continued to flow through his hands. Abraham could no longer afford to be associated with street business of any kind. He had planned on running for Alderman during Macon's freshman year at college, and his hard headed ass had almost messed that up. Abraham had dreams of being the city's second black mayor, and he wasn't about to let Macon fuck that up.

"Man I feel like I'm seeing you off to college again." Terry joked as Macon got out of the car to greet him.

They had decided to meet at an apartment building that Abraham owned on Kostner and 14th. It was a nice building with six apartments that

47

brought in a steady income, legal and illegal. Technically, apartment 3C was being rented to Ms. Grace Dawson, but it was really just a cover for one of the places they stashed their products and collected money. If there was a Grace Dawson, they certainly didn't know her.

"So you ready to jump the broom and get out the game?" Terry asked Macon, locking the apartment door behind him.

"Man she is the one, every king needs a queen. Besides she will be the picture perfect wife when I put in my bid to run for a city office." Macon bragged. "I need to get out the game while I'm still ahead. Finally listen to my daddy I guess." He chuckled.

"He always has good advice." Terry had to admit.

He'd come to him on many occasions for advice and guidance and he had yet to steer him wrong.

"It's time to grow up and get this legit paper man. I want a family with Denise and these young cats don't respect the game like it should be."

Macon knew it was time to hang up his guns. These new hustlers, or dope boys, were too thirsty, thirsty for money, power, and street fame. They had no rules they followed, and no boundaries. It seemed in this day and age, loyalty was for suckers. Macon was just lucky he made it out unscathed. He just hoped that his best friend, Terry, would be able to do the same.

After talking for a while and having a congratulatory drink or two, Macon got up to leave.

"Let me get to Denise man, she claims we need to have a talk before we go out to dinner."

"Uh oh, every time they say talk, it either involves a lot of cash, or you about to get cussed out." Terry said playfully. "You will still end up coming out of a lot of cash in the end."

Giving his friend dap Macon made his way home to Denise, to his future.

When Macon got home he went to the bedroom being drawn by sounds coming from that way. It almost sounded like someone was crying.

"Denise," he called out, "you alright baby?"

"I'm in the room come back here."

She sounded like something was distressing her, he was beginning to worry something was really wrong. When he entered the room, he found her not on the bed where he expected, but in the closet; on her knees trying to figure out the combination to his safe. Before he could breathe an inward sigh of relief she was on him.

"What is so important that you need to hide it from me?" She questioned. "Why the secrets; what are you hiding Macon? Are you, are you selling drugs Macon?"

Macon's heart dropped into his stomach. How could she have deduced that by just seeing a safe in the closet? He had been very careful to keep the street business away from her. The only person she knew tied remotely to it was Terry, and Macon knew he didn't say anything.

"You're probably wondering where that came from?" Denise said looking him in his eye for any signs of betrayal. "The money, the expensive trips, the jewels, furs, all of it doesn't add up. In the time we have been together you've spent ten times what your legit check reflects, did you think I couldn't catch on?"

"Baby that safe is not what you think..." Macon began, knowing that just hours earlier it had been filled with his last three kilos of coke.

The only thing remaining in there were important papers and Denise's engagement ring. There were many times he wanted to admit to the woman he loved what he really did for cash. The college degree and political aspirations were a front to keep his family's most lucrative, illegal business running smoothly. In Chicago, political power was everything. Money didn't mean shit if you didn't play the politics game.

"Well open the safe then." Denise said deadpan.

As Macon leaned down to unlock the safe, he chuckle to himself as he thought, *this is definitely not the proposal I had in mind.*

"Oh you think this shit is funny?" Denise asked hearing his laughter, as he opened the sage.

Macon reached in to pull out the box that contained her engagement ring out, its total weight was five karats, with the centre stone being a three karat square cut diamond mounted in a band that was encircled in stones that made up the rest of the weight.

"What are you trying to hide why? You leaning over the safe and shit?"

When Macon turned around and Denise saw the purple velvet box, her mouth hung open and a tear formed in her eye.

"I can't believe...I'm so sorry." She wept, reaching out to hug Macon.

"So, I'll take that as a yes?" He said laughing.

"You damn right it's a yes!" Denise said as he slipped the ring on the finger.

"This means life. Forever. Unconditional love and loyalty, those are the ties that bind a family." He said looking into her eyes. "Are you ready to be a family?"

Denise had to laugh at that, "We're a family alright, maybe a lot sooner than either one of us ever thought." She said placing his hand on her stomach. "Might as well make it official."

About two months later, they were married in a beautiful ceremony at a church in the northwest suburbs of Chicago. There were about two hundred and fifty guest at their wedding, many of them Denise only knew through stories told by her father-in-law and all were very gracious when it came time to fill the wishing well up at the wedding. There were also a few faces that she was surprised to see, and a few questionable associates of Abrahams also in attendance. A few of them being known for being associated with questionable characters. Although they acted the perfect gentleman and even danced with her. Denise couldn't help but to wonder if

Macon had been lying about being a drug dealer. She quickly shook the thought aside as her new father-in-law took her hand to dance.

"Denise you look beautiful in that dress." Abraham complimented her.

Her father-in-law's approval was important to her, but not quite as much as it was to Macon. He didn't even let Abraham know they were getting married until after they had set a date. His father didn't personally have anything against Denise, but he wanted to make sure his son married a woman who understood what the word family meant. Loyalty until death is what it meant to Abraham and anyone let into that tight circle he called family had to be thorough thru and thru, his son's new wife was no exception.

"Thank you" Denise blushed. "And I would also like to thank you for the beautiful pearl necklace of your wife's you allowed me the honour of wearing today."

Denise didn't know how she felt about Abraham. It seemed like he was always watching, observing, waiting for her to do something that he disapproved of. Although Abraham had never mistreated her or been ungracious, she got the feeling she would never be good enough for Macon, let alone him.

"Those are yours to keep. If Macon's mother were alive, I am sure she would love for you to have them. Think of them as a family heirloom you will pass on to my granddaughter one day." He said, keeping in step with the music from the jazz band playing in the background.

Denise sensed he had more to say or was trying to feel her out. Before she could reply he continued.

"Tradition and family are very important to me, to us; Macon and me. We are attempting to build a family legacy in this city to rival that of the Daley's. This is a family venture and everyone must be on board for it to work." Abraham said, leading her off the dance floor and back to the handsome groom.

Denise didn't know what he expected her to say. Was that a veiled threat, or a welcome to the family speech? It sounded like a little of both to her. What did he mean by that?

"Thank you for returning my beautiful wife." Macon said, as he took Denise's hand from his father.

The night went on and all the guest raved at what a lovely time they had at the wedding. By the end of the night Denise was exhausted, her feet hurt and her dress was way too tight. The little baby nestling in her womb felt like he had grown in the few hours of the wedding.

As Denise and Macon sat on their king sized be in the presidential suit of the Palmer House Hotel, they counted up well over ten thousand dollars in their wishing well from the wedding. Denise was floored.

"Who has hundreds of dollars to give away to someone they barely even know?" She said aloud to no one in particular.

"Get used to it baby." Macon said "The bigger the gift they sent us, the larger the favour they expect from my father. It's all politics baby; no one in this city does something for nothing, and there is no reason why my wife and son shouldn't prosper."

"Who said the baby was a he?" Denise said playfully.

"Well if he isn't a boy now, I'll have fun making my son the next time around."

They shared a laugh, finished counting their money and set goals, and plans for the life they had ahead. Almost seven months to the day Macon Jr, better known as Mako was born.

CHAPTER 5

Fathers

"Where the hell is that damn boy?" Abraham cursed Mako out loud.

He had a very important meeting with some city planners in about an hour and he had let Mako know for the last month he wanted him to attend so could learn the family trade, politics. Abraham knew Mako wasn't interested in being involved in politics or anything else for that matter. It seemed that this generation was more into being a gangsta and wearing it like a badge than becoming a businessman. These kids now days were dumb as shit and had no respect for the game whatsoever. They didn't understand the sacrifices their parents, grandparents, and great-grand parents went through to make sure their ungrateful asses had the opportunity to get a decent education, living wage and housing. Now look at the shit.

As Abraham sat in the backseat of his Cadillac STS, his driver asked if he was speaking to him.

"No Tony, I was speaking out loud about Mako and his refusal to act right."

Tony started laughing, "Okay sir." He responded.

He had known Mako since he was a little boy and he always was a little slick. Tony had helped him get out of more jams than he could remember, but he always hooked Tony up in the end.

As they drove on the expressway towards their destination, Abraham instructed Tony to take the streets so he could see the old neighbourhood. Tony did as he was told, but Abraham quickly regretted his decision once he saw how much the city was changing. As Tony drove down Madison, Abraham's heart sank. He couldn't believe this used to be his stomping ground. What was once an avenue filled with storefronts, with respectable owners who kept up their property, sweeping out front, washing their windows, taking pride in what they owned were long gone.

The sidewalks were littered with trash, as if the people didn't notice the city provided wire mesh garbage cans on every corner. You would think they stayed full the way people littered on the ground. There were prostitutes out, in broad daylight with random body parts on display to entice whoever was buying, and of course there were hypes out. They were always out looking for a fix. No inner city neighbourhood would be complete without them. There were groups of young abled bodied men, just idling on corners doing God knows what. Abraham shook his head.

"This is what the city of my youth has become? A fantasyland for prostitutes, hypes, and dope dealers. My people, my people, we need to do better." Abraham thought as memories began to flood his mind.

He remembered the first time he saw Chicago and how awestruck of a southern Mississippi boy he was at how black people were dressed to the nines, drove fancy cars and had money in their pocket. To him this was unheard of. A black man in Mississippi was not able to show his wealth openly, if he had it, for fear that some white man would trick him out of it, or just kill him for having more with no consequences. No this, place is where a black man's dreams could come true and the young fresh faced, naïve Abraham Clark was determined to succeed.

It was the summer of 1938 when Abraham Clark stepped off the train that brought him from a little sharecropping plantation located outside of Hattiesburg, Mississippi and into the black Promised Land, Chicago. Up until three days prior, Abraham had never been out of Hattiesburg, let alone Mississippi. However, the racial tension, mindless lynching of black men, and women in some instances too made his overworked sharecropping parents beg, borrow, and scrape for train fare to send their only son to Chicago. His parents knew that the south would never allow their son to become a man, whether in age or respectability, and this was the only opportunity they could offer.

His father's sister Clancy had been there for about ten years and had found a good man and decent job. His Auntie Clancy had been the first in the family to depart the dirt roads of Mississippi and she had never looked back. A car horn brought Abraham back to earth.

"Is that my nephew?" Clancy called out.

She had pulled up in a bright red Series 60 Cadillac convertible. As she embraced her nephew in a hug, he took in the sweet scent of her perfume, something expensive probably to match with this car he thought.

"Let me look at you son!" She said holding him at arm's length to get a good look.

At sixteen years old, Abraham had the well-developed muscles of a hardworking man, with calloused hands to go along with it. He stood about five foot eleven at that time with broad shoulders, a bright inviting smile and skin the color of a ginger snap.

Giving him the once over Clancy said, "Now you are just as handsome as my big brother sho nuff, but those overalls have got to go nephew."

Abraham's smile quickly left as he realized he looked like a country bumpkin surrounded by all these city folks. Seeing the hurt in his eyes, Clancy reassured him.

"Hey don't worry yourself, when I first got off that bus all I had was two dresses that were hand me downs and I was wearing one of em! Now look at me." She said letting her nephew take in her beautifully fitting, black, gathered skirt, red shirt with matching *sweater and even redder lipstick. She was gorgeous and looked like she was rich.*

"I'm gonna take you shopping nephew, we are gonna have so much fun. Chicago ain't nothing like Mississippi, we can do whatever we want and go wherever we want just about. We can even sit in the front row and watch a picture show! Things are different, but you'll fit in." Clancy said, hugging him one more time and getting into the car.

Abraham got into the passenger side of the car he thought one day he could someone day have one just like it. Finally, somewhere a black man could be a MAN. He knew him and Chicago would get along just fine.

Clancy lived in the Western part of North Lawndale, known as K-town. Historically, it received its name because all the streets started with the letter K. However, as time would move forward, the K in K-town had begun to stand for the word killer. Back then it was still a fairly nice neighbourhood. Many black people owned stores and shops in the area and those who could afford it began to buy homes in the community. Lawndale had started out as a nice Jewish community, but as the blacks in the city began to be displaced, due to city construction projects, they had moved to the western edge of Lawndale in droves.

Many middle class, upwardly mobile blacks wanted the chance to buy into the American dream, and there weren't too many nice neighbourhoods that would accept blacks with open arms. It may have been the north, but there was a different form of racism practiced here. In the South a black man knew where he was not welcome or accepted, hell he didn't need the white only signs to let him know that, but up here, the white people treated you kindly enough, but still thought you were inferior. No one said outwardly nigger you can't live here, but the ever changing city district lines and the neighbourhoods where black families were run out of let you know that as much a things changed, they had still stayed the same.

Those first few weeks in the city, Abraham stuck out like a sore thumb, even though Clancy had him dress the part, his naïve smile and trusting nature made him instant prey on the streets of Chicago. He was there less than two weeks when he began to think living in Chicago wasn't all bread and roses. Clancy had to go into work and needed him to go to the corner store to get some milk and eggs so she could finish making her cornbread. She had let him out the apartment, but never without her or her boyfriend Freddy, Fabulous, as he was known on the streets. She knew that those streets would chew him up and spit him out, like they had tried to do her upon her arrival to the big city, but she needed him to hurry up so she could get to work. She was late a few times last week and didn't want to hear the prejudice ass head of nursing talking shit again.

"Look, go to the store and come right back, so I can fix the supper and get on out of here." She said, gathering up the other ingredients for her cornbread.

Although the corner store was three blocks away, a lot of dangers for a country boy lay within those three blocks. He came in contact with pimps, hookers, hustlers, and even some guys playing dice in the alley. He tried not to stare too long at all these things that were filling his senses. It made him look green, his auntie's boyfriend had told him.

"Look young blood, I'm gonna hip you to some game. Stop smiling and speaking to every nigga you pass in the street. You are just drawing attention to yourself." He said with red rimmed eyes and faint traces of liquor on his breath.

"I'm just being polite, good manners and all." Abraham said, feeling ashamed for the first time in his life to be mannerable.

Freddie laughed, "Being polite will get your little bumpkin ass shook. Trust me, when you smile at someone you know they are thinking one of two things; who the fuck is this nigga, and what do he want. Put people on the defence."

"You ain't in Mississippi no more, the game here is offence."

"Leave my nephew alone Freddie." Clancy said.

Although she knew Freddy was right, she didn't want him to erase. all the good upbringing she knew Abraham had. It was tough living in the city, but her nephew was smarter than he looked. He would stay away from trouble she hoped, knowing how powerful the lure of money, women, and a little bit of fame in the neighbourhood could go to a black man's head. Just look at Freddy, "Fabulous" as he was now called, he went from being blue collar worker, with a highly coveted city job, and tossed it away for fast money with no benefits.

Abraham made it to the store without incident, it was on his way back that he encountered a little trouble. The same guys that had been shooting dice in the alley had now turned their attention to a young man who looked to be no more than Abraham's age.

"Yo Charlie!" One of the dice players called out.

When the kid looked up to see who had called his name, he started to break out in a run. Abraham was sure he had just missed something. All the, man did was call the boy's name and he scattered. Abraham moved out the way as the Charlie started running in his direction. When the man finally caught up with him at the end of the block, it was only because the boy had tripped on his shoelaces, he instantly began laying into him.

"Hey little man what ya running for? I ain't gonna hurt you. I just want to know where to find that sister of yours. She has something that belongs to me."

The man who had chased Charlie down was known in the neighbourhood as Nookie. He got the name because he was fine as hell and was always getting the goods from the hottest chicks. Nookie was also a small time drug dealer and pimp. He was looking for Charlie's older sister, Myra, because she had stolen some dope and money from him after he had beaten her for not wanting to sell her body for him anymore.

"I haven't seen Myra." Charlie stammered. "I don't know where she is."

"I think you might have a clue, she is your sister. Now tell me where that bitch is or I'm gonna beat your little ass until you do." He said looking Charlie in his eye.

To be honest, he had no clue where his sister was. He hadn't seen her in months, ever since this slick talking chump had turned her out to drugs and selling pussy. Every now and then he would catch glimpses of his sister getting in or out of cars, or coming out the dope house, but he never spoke. He didn't know what to say to her, or how to say it. Even if he did know where she was, he would never tell Nookie. Wherever she was, he just hoped she was safe and not on drugs or selling cat.

The vicious slap to his face from Nookie brought him out of his thoughts. Dragging him in the gangway between two buildings, Nookie proceeded to beat the child into a confession. He didn't care that he was a grown man and this was a teenager. All he knew was that his top ass seller cut out with a lot of money and some dope he had gotten on credit. Shit, Fabulous didn't play about his money and after dodging him for weeks, it was time to pay the piper.

Finally realizing that either the kid knew nothing or was saying nothing, Nookie pulled out his switchblade and put it up to Charlie's throat.

"This is my last time asking you kid, where she at?" He said pressing the knife to the corner of Charlie's eye.

His face was so bloody that it looked like he was crying tears of blood. Charlie close his eyes hoping that the pain wouldn't be too bad. He'd had worse beatings from his father on a drunken night, but he had never knifed out his eye or threatened to. Before Charlie's thoughts could go any further, a loud sound caught his attention, and he noticed the grip Nookie had on him slip away until he finally fell to the ground. Charlie collapsed too. His body was sore, bruised and broken and he could already feel the swelling in his face. He was going to have a really bad black eye.

"Are you okay man? Hey can you hear me?" The voice of Charlie's saviour called out.

All he could do was moan in response, but that was enough for the stranger who dropped his grocery bag and scooped Charlie up in its place.

"Can you walk?" He asked. "You gotta help me a little, when can get to my house through the alley if you can just hold on."

Charlie was so grateful, for a moment he had thought he was going to die in the gutter the way so many other black folks had. No one there to care, no one there to help. People on the street had seen what was going down, yet no one stepped in, what they did was step over him and keep going. Damn shame.

"Where have you been?" His auntie called out when she heard the front open. "I thought something had happened to you." She stopped her words when she saw what Abraham had dragged in the door.

"Oh my God, what happened!?" She asked in shock. "Who is this boy? Who did this to him?" Clancy immediately went into nurse mode telling Abraham to get water, towels, the first aid kit, and Freddy from the back room. "But make sure you knock first!" Clancy called out down the hallway.

The backroom was right off the kitchen, it wasn't quite big enough to be a bedroom, but was too big to be considered a pantry.

Many people used this room as a bedroom for overflow family members when necessary, but right now it was Freddy's office.

After collecting Freddy and the supplies for his auntie, Abraham made it to the front of the house. By the time Clancy cleaned him up, Charlie didn't look that bad. Sure he had a shiner and a few bruises, scrapes, and cuts, but he would live and that is truly what mattered.

"Listen with all this commotion, I'm gonna be late for work!" Clancy declared. "Let me get on my way, before I get fired." She said kissing both Abraham and Freddy on the forehead.

"Now Charlie baby, you stay here until you feel safe okay? Where are your parents, at work?" Charlie was too ashamed to admit where his parent truly were. His momma was long dead and his daddy was probably in someone's bar or whorehouse, but he didn't want to tell this nice lady that.

"Yes ma'am," he quickly answered, "they're at work right now."

Something in Clancy let her know this boy most likely didn't have any comfort at home, so she insisted he at least get some supper before he left. Once Clancy left out the door, Freddy started in.

"Alright young blood now that Clancy is gone, tell me the real story. Not that bullshit you threw her about getting jumped for a few dollars. I can look at you and tell you ain't got a dollar, let alone a few." He said suspiciously.

Freddy's hard stare made Charlie break under the pressure as he told him the true story. When Charlie laid it out, he was overcome with a range of emotions for his sister and that bum Nookie. At the mention of Nookie's name Fabulous' ears perked up. That nigga had been dodging him and now he knew why. The dumb ass had let some young girl take him for his money and Fabulous' dope. He had every excuse in the book, now he had the real reason, but it wasn't good

61

enough. Now he had beat the breaks off this kid, what good was that gonna do?

"Nookie huh? Don't worry about Nookie, I'll take care of that for you my man, as for your sister, I'm sorry I can't help you there." Fabulous said feeling sorry for the kid. He had seen it too many times, pretty girl in the hood swept off their feet by some punk ass pimp who hooks them on dope to keep his money flowing. He knew the story all too well, his mother had been one of those women.

That day a bond had been created, a friend found, a brother gained. From that day forward, Abraham Clark and Charles "Charlie" Johnson were as thick as thieves and best friends. Charlie helped Abraham's transition from a country boy to a city kid a little smoother, and Abraham helped Charlie to see that family does not always carry blood ties.

The vibration of Abraham's phone shook him out of his memories. Looking at the caller id he saw it was his grandson.

"It's about damn time." He said to himself. "Macon, I hope you are calling me to tell me you are either on your way or already at UIC for the hearing."

"Yes, Granddad, I'm on my way." Mako said, sounding bored.

"You don't seem too worried about your fate Macon," he said irritably. "We both know that with this mess you have caused your future, as well as mine hangs in the balance. So have a little respect and gratitude for the opportunities you have been afforded in life."

Blah, blah, blah. How many times had Mako heard this speech, too many to count? Here we go again.

"I'm just saying Pops, my academic record at the school is outstanding, I am about to graduate valedictorian of the school of business management. Up until now, I have never had an infraction on my record. This is no biggie." Mako shrugged the situation off.

In actuality, the situation, or infraction was a huge biggie. Mako's named had been implicated when an arrest was made in one of the dorms during a room inspection when one of the RA's noticed an illegal cooking appliance box in the student's room. He found it full of weed, pills, and even a little coke. The student had been a white kid on a scholarship who was trying to make extra money. He had been supplying the dorm with drugs and he wasn't the only one. Threatened with jail time, he spilled his guts and named everyone he could possibly think of. Although he didn't know Mako, nor had never met him, the name of one of the people he had given mentioned a name that was associated with him.

Abraham was furious at his grandsons nonchalant attitude about being kicked out of school so close to graduation, after he had laid such careful plans over the years to ensure a political family dynasty in Chicago, and eventually the state of Illinois. He had to choke back the words he really wanted to say.

"Just be there on time." He said, hanging up before Mako could respond.

Unlike his grandfather, Mako was not worried about the disciplinary board or any of its members. His grandfather had taught him well, Mako had dirt not only on the dean, but a few faculty members on the board as well. Mako supplied the dean with plenty of coke once he found his weakness. Two of the faculty members who taught classes Mako had aced, were known to have sex with students, and unbeknownst to them Mako had even managed to get them on tape. One of the only other black students that excelled in his major happened to be a fine sister, who stripped at night to pay her way through school. Mako used it to his advantage by setting up the faculty member, and dean as well. He paid her handsomely, and she climbed off the pole faster than you could blink.

Once he realized that college students got just as high as neighbourhood dope fiends, with plenty of mommy and daddy's money to spend, he couldn't resist. He knew he was there to get an education, but he figured he could get a street education as well as a mainstream education. Before long Mako had it on and popping with various workers scattered throughout the dorm buildings. It had been his best buddy Timmo's plan to flood the campus and get all the profit. Mako smiled inwardly as he thought about what a great idea his friend had. Within a few months, they had enough money and clientele to compare to a big time street hustler. Except here, as long as you stayed on your shit, you didn't need to worry about the punk ass campus police. Especially him, some of them were on Mako's payroll too.

Besides, Mako knew Abraham would do whatever it took to stop his image from being tarnished. He had aspirations for being the governor one day, and he would nothing or no one stop him. So he knew if his insurance wasn't enough to cash in Abraham would do the rest. Mako was going to walk out of here and graduate on Saturday afternoon with honours in the college of Business Management, as well as wearing the sash that showed he was valedictorian just like his grandfather, no one was going to stop him.

The hearing lasted about twenty minutes before the board decided there was no concrete evidence that tied Mako to any wrong doing. Mako left with a smug look on his face, and Abraham left without having to call in any favours.

"You need to wipe that smirk off your face Macon, at least wait until you get to your car to gloat."

Abraham thought the boy had no tact sometimes. Texting on his phone for a part of the short meeting, being blatantly disrespectful, Abraham could only think what favours it would cost this time to clean up behind his grandson. One day Mako was going to get into something that Abraham wouldn't be able to pay for or cover up or get him out of. He just hoped that day didn't come soon.

64

"Pops you don't look like the proud grandfather of a college graduate, with honours I might add." Mako replied shrugging off the seriousness of the situation.

If Mako knew how angry his grandfather really was, he would not have joked with him. Grabbing Mako's arm, Abraham spoke in a serious, sincere tone.

"Macon you and your wellbeing are very important to me. After your father died I realized you were the only living family I had left, and I would protect you at all cost, but son I'm at the point where I believe you are manipulating the bond we share."

Mako looked at his grandfather puzzled, Pops had always lectured, but it was something about these words that seemed ominous to Mako, like his grandfather was giving him an ultimatum. Get your shit together or I am cutting all ties.

"Pops, I got you." Mako said trying to appease Abraham. "I know I've been a little buck lately but after Saturday, I become a man and I will put all childish things away." He said throwing in that biblical quote.

Abraham gave him the evil eye as he got into the backseat of his car.

"No more Macon today is it." He said, before slamming the door and ordering Tony to pull away.

"It's like that?" Mako thought hopping into his Impala. His granddad was really tripping, no harm no foul, right?

CHAPTER 6

Opportunity Comes Knocking

"Where you at ma?" Mako asked Tasha through the Bluetooth head piece he had on.

"Why, you keeping tabs on me?" Tasha asked playfully.

"I always keep tabs on hot commodities these days. Naw, I was trying to ride down on you, take you to a late lunch, maybe a little shopping."

It didn't take Tasha long to reply, "That's cool but let me tell you now I don't have an Applebee's kind of appetite boo, and I definitely don't shop on the ave." She said playfully but in a way to know she was dead ass serious.

"Look game recognizes game. The way you walked, talked, dressed and carried yourself the first time I met you let me know from the jump you only accept the best, and that's good because that is all I have to offer." Mako said.

"Alright, it sounds good." Tasha said. "So when you coming to scoop me, my wheels ain't right at this moment. I'm out south in the hundreds, what's your location?"

"I'm out west."

"Out west, I would have never guessed. Those niggas out there so damn grimy. They will kill they momma for a blow." She laughed.

"Man I know you ain't talking, them niggas from the hundreds wild as hell! Why you think they call it the Wild 100's?" Mako shot back.

"Yeah whatever." Tasha said, "Now that you know where I live, you still coming or what. You know how y'all dudes act like the west and south is two different countries, always at war."

"I'll be there in about an hour so get ready ma."

Mako did think twice about going out there alone, so before hanging up on Tasha, he told her to grab a friend because Timmo was with him. She was forced to call Kristen because Jaleesa had to work and she wasn't missing her paper for nobody. Once she told Kristen what was up, she was knocking at her door before she could hang up the phone good.

"Girl open the door." Kristen said hollering as she rang the bell. "You knew I was coming, I'm only across the street."

"Why can't this hoe ever act right?" Tasha sighed to herself as she opened the door. "Man you rushing over here like you dressed or something you still got on night clothes." Tasha scolded.

"Girl I just got out the tub a few minutes ago and I ain't got shit clean to wear."

"Okay, and?" Tasha said.

She already knew what Kristen was on, trying to squeeze that big ass of hers in some designer wear. Shit, he big sister managed the Laundromat/dry cleaners on 111th, there wasn't a good reason why she shouldn't have at least one off the rack Baby Phat outfit to wear.

"Man why you acting like that?" Kristen said, turning up her nose. "I live right across the street you gonna get whatever I borrow back."

"Yeah right." Tasha mumbled under her breath as she opened the door for Kristen to let her in.

It seemed like the older they got, the less she wanted Kristen over there. She was always commenting on how much everything probably cost, and asking way too many questions about her uncles' business. Tasha wasn't naïve, and neither had Raymond or Charles wanted her to be. They let their niece know what was up, where the bulk of the cash came from, and most importantly to be aware at all times. They knew danger might fall on her head because of their life style, so they taught her to protect herself and family at all cost.

Whatever outfit she loaned Kristen, she would never see again. She wasn't really into the clothes borrowing trend, really none of her friends had anything she wanted to rock, and if they did, she would cop her own. She was a spoiled brat. She knew it and so did everyone else. That caused eyes of admiration, as well as envy to be on her at all times. She used to think Kristen looked at her with eyes of admiration, but now that they were young women, she wasn't too sure anymore.

"Kris, I don't know why you believe I am your personal shopper and what's in my closet belongs to you. You got more close than closet room across the street." Tasha quipped, letting her know she was tired of this shit.

"Don't be like that T. I'm just trying to be as fly as you, since you and Jaleesa treat me like a common hood rat." Kristen threw in to pull on Tasha's heartstrings.

She knew that Jaleesa thought she was better than her and let her know it at all times, and when all three were together, she always felt like she didn't fit in, like she wasn't on their level, at least Tasha's.

That stung Tasha a little bit because she had always tried to include Kristen in things she did with Jaleesa so she wouldn't feel like a second hand friend. She was always hooking Kristen up, especially on her birthdays. She loved Kristen, she just did not share the same bond she had with Jaleesa. In some ways Tasha felt like they were sisters, or blood related. There were some slight resemblances in some of their facial features that made you look twice. Yet they always wrote it off with the old saying, if you are with someone enough you start to look like them.

"Oh Krissy," Tasha said shaking her head, "I'm sure you know your way to the mini mall." Tasha said referring to her closet that was always filled with the newest fashions.

"Thanks." Kristen smirked, making her way to Tasha's room.

To call it a room would actually be an understatement. When Charles and Raymond had decided to refurbish the three flat building they grew up in, they spared no expense in making sure it was laid out in luxury. The first and second floor apartments had been combined to make on large apartment, reminiscent of the refurbished brownstones down on 43rd. The first floor consisted of a kitchen, den, dining room, a small office and a spare room.

The second floor was jokingly referred to as Tasha's palace. This floor consisted of four bedrooms, one belonging to each of the twins and two belonging to Tasha. The smaller of the rooms had been converted into Tasha's wardrobe, to house all of the shoes, purses, and outfits she had collected over the years. The twins had spent ten thousand alone paying for the installation of a custom made closet, with special racks for her shoes, purses, and sweaters that were kept pristine in a climate controlled environment.

"Damn, look like somebody went shopping." Kristen said as she pawed her way through the clothes in Tasha's closet.

"Just hurry up and find something, Mako will be here in about an hour." Tasha said leaving Kristen in the closet, and returning to finish getting ready. After about fifteen minutes, Kristen had decided on an outfit. When she brought it to Tasha for her approval, she quickly shook her head at the Baby Phat outfit she chose.

"We're going somewhere classy Kristen. You definitely gonna look like you don't belong in that outfit."

"Try on that cream matte jersey Donna Karen dress that hangs off the shoulders. It's a little bit too loose for me around the waist, seeing as I don't have all that ass you do." Tasha said playfully smacking Kristen on her big round ass.

Kristen was about to ask Tasha what was wrong with her choice of outfit, but thought better of it. Tasha was just trying to look out for her she reasoned. She didn't want her to stick out or feel like she didn't belong. Deciding she would not only keep the dress but the Baby Phat outfit to cheer her up.

"And then let me do your make up when you get dressed." Tasha added, knowing the right amount of make-up would accentuate Kristen's pretty face.

She definitely knew that dress would accentuate every curve and crevice she had. Maybe she could finally attract the attention of a real baller.

When Mako pulled up in front of Tasha's building, he was somewhat surprised. When he got off the Dan Ryan e-way on 111th, the ever present poverty of Chicago's Southside invaded his senses. He had expected Tasha's house to be raggedy like almost every other inner city property in Chicago. So when he turned off Michigan Avenue and pulled up in front of a gleaming brick three flat in one of the city's worst neighbourhoods, he was caught off guard. He could tell that whoever owned the building had cared enough about their property to keep it up. He bet the rent in that mofo was sky high, but with all these Section 8 vouchers going around, he could find someone to cover the rent.

"Damn man," Timmo remarked, "that building looks so out of place on this block, almost like it don't belong."

"I know right?" Mako replied, as Tasha and Kristen came out the front door to the building.

A few people outside commented on how nice they looked and where they were going, and of course with who. That was a new vehicle in the premises and some new niggas and everyone was just being nosy. Tasha brushed them off, as Timmo got out of the front seat to let her in.

"So where we going for lunch?" Tasha asked. "I told you I don't do Applebee's." She joked.

"Naw," Mako laughed, "we are going to an Italian spot downtown called the Italian Village. Then I figured I would treat you to a little shopping on the magnificent mile."

"Well if that's the case, I say we shop first, it always helps me work up an appetite." Tasha chuckled.

Kristen sat in the backseat with Timmo who was trying to make small talk. Timmo hadn't really wanted to ride but when Mako told him the girl with the fat ass was riding, he couldn't resist missing a chance to get in that ass. Mako had told him they were gonna take the girls out to lunch, but he didn't say shit about splurging no money on these hoes. It wasn't that Timmo was stingy, but he wasn't giving a bitch shit without her spreading those legs first. He had to make sure the pussy was worth the payment, and he damn sure wasn't about to change today for Kristen, who seemed to be paying more attention to Mako in the rear-view mirror than the game he was spitting.

Lunch turned out to be really good, but the shopping turned out to be even better. However, Mako and Timmo stopped for a side bar in the Levi store to talk as the girls tried on jeans. Timmo was not cool with the fact he was expected to spend money on this broad, and Mako knowing his friend so well, hit him off with a grand just for riding along. With the understanding that it was to get in with the friend so he could get in with Tasha.

71

"Tasha is a classy chick fam. She pays attention to shit like that. If you don't kick her friend down, she is going to think I'm as stingy as you." Mako said, laughing while handing Timmo a wad of cash on the sly.

Kristen caught the transaction as she was coming out of the dressing room.

"Damn, why did he bring a broke ass nigga with him." She thought.

The nigga Timmo looked caked up, but she thought he was just a flunky. The more Kristen thought about the situation the more upset she became.

"Oh so that's what you think of me Tasha?" She thought while bringing her items to the counter to purchase. "A low budget hood chick that only deserves handouts?"

Kristen was brought out of the rager by Timmo telling her to come on so he could pay for her things. While standing at the counter she couldn't help but to notice how cute Tasha and Mako looked together. She could see Mako was digging Tasha and vice versa. She decided as the clerk handed her bags that she would have everything Tasha had, wanted and then some. She just needed to figure out how to do it.

"Now where these sluts at?" Jaleesa thought to herself as she rang Tasha's bell for the umpteenth time.

She had already gone across the street to see if they were at Kristen's house, but her sister Samantha said she hadn't seen her, she had been working at the cleaners all day. It was 7 pm and Jaleesa was ready to get it in. She had worked all day with those bad ass kids at the day care and she needed a drink and a blunt to unwind.

"Hugh!" She said jamming the doorbell hard one last time before heading off the porch to Zach's to grab a half pint and a Vega. As Jaleesa was walking into the liquor store, Mako was pulling up in front of Tasha's house.

"So did you enjoy your afternoon out Ms. Lady?" Mako teased Tasha.

"I sure did. My stomach and closet thank you very much."

Tasha and Mako had been back and forth all day with that flirtatious conversational tone. It made Kristen want to puke and also made Timmo uncomfortable, knowing neither him nor Kristen really wanted to be in the car with them any longer.

"Alright let me get your stuff out the trunk." Mako said unlatching the trunk and getting out.

That was Kristen's cue, "Look Timmo, I know this day turned out to be uncomfortable for us both, but maybe one on one it would be better, put my number in your phone." Kristen flirted.

Timmo was kind of surprised by the offer but took her number anyway. You know what they say, the best pussy is new pussy, and he would definitely give that a go. Little did Timmo know Kristen had been forming a plan the whole ride back to the Southside, and he would play a crucial part in it. He would allow her to get closer to Mako, which in turn would allow her the chance to let Tasha know she was just as valuable as her. She didn't care if she ended up losing a friend. Get the man, and get the money were her goals. Once she rode off into the sunset with her baller, what would she need Tasha for? She had always played Kristen to the left for that stuck up bitch Jaleesa anyway.

Oh yes, this would work out perfectly. Kristen had yet to meet a man who could resist the sex game she threw down. She did everything, including threesomes. Yet she didn't have shit to show for

73

it but a raggedy ass car, she had to steal back. No this time she would take Tasha's advice and upgrade, to know her worth and demand it from a nigga. She planned on upgrading with Mako. She knew her worth could be found somewhere in the depths of his pockets.

"What up Le Le?" Juicy said sliding up next to her as she paid for her blunt and bottle at the counter.

"What up, are you paying for my purchase?" Jaleesa joked. Before she could get her chuckle out good, Juicy pulled a wad of cash out his pocket and hand her forty dollars, knowing good and well her bill was less than twenty.

"Can I keep the change too?" Jaleesa replied putting the money in her pocket. "Good looking Juice."

Shit a penny saved is a penny earned, and since Jaleesa wasn't messing with any dudes at the time, she was living off her own pay checks. By the time she was through spending what she pleased and putting money aside for her future college dreams, all she had left was car fare to make it to work until the next payday. Juicy had just brought her a bus pass for the next two weeks.

"Where you running off too?" Juicy asked as he walked out of Zach's with Jaleesa.

"Why you want to know?" She teased. "You trying to take me out?"

"Not yet. I gotta get my money right for you baby girl." He joked, but inside he was dead serious.

Juicy had been crushing on Jaleesa since they were shorties. And when she moved off the block he was devastated. She didn't start coming back to hang around until a few years ago, when her momma loosened the leash she had on her. Lena never wanted Jaleesa hanging on that block, knowing the dangers that lurked everywhere.

74

Lena also knew that Jaleesa's destination on the block was a building that held many memories for her, happy as well as sad. She just did not want her daughter to get caught up in the streets like her best friend had. It would crush Lena if anything happened to her.

When Jaleesa turned seventeen, Lena started working later hours at work and more, knowing she was going to pay for a college education soon. Jaleesa took to running the streets behind her mother's back. Coming to the hood when Lena was at work to hang out on the block. Once Charles and Raymond began to notice her presence in the hood more often than not, Raymond called Lena and told her Jaleesa had been sneaking over there when she was at work. Raymond felt the same way for Jaleesa as Lena did. He didn't want Tasha around there either, but as her legal guardian she went where he went, and when they tried to move out of the building into a better neighbourhood and house Tasha refused, cried pleaded, and begged to at least let her grow up where her mother did, it was all she had left.

That did it for Raymond, he paid the penalties on the cancelled housing contracts and redid the house to please Tasha. The guilt of what had happened would not allow him to deny her that one request; yet the walls and furniture that held Jackie's laughter and good memories ate away at him every day, every night. That's why he was hardly ever there. That is why he redid the house, to erase the haunting memories of Jackie, and to please Tasha.

"Well I was going to kick it with T and see what she was up to, but she ain't answer the door."

"I saw her and Kristen cut out earlier with some nigga with dreads and a short stocky guy." Juicy told her. "I been out for a minute and haven't seen them roll back around this way yet. So let's grab a sack, pop that bottle and chill at the spot." Juicy suggested.

"Juicy," Jaleesa began, "I ain't on that shit! You know I don't bust down boo!" She laughed.

"Damn Le Le it ain't like that, I just figured you might as well kick it with me while you wait on ya girls to roll back through here. Why a nigga always gotta be trying to fuck?" Juicy asked annoyed.

He had never looked at Jaleesa like a jump off. If anything she was a million steps above these bum ass bitches around her, with the exception of Tasha. All these chicks were looking for was the next baller to be their baby daddy, or buy them some gym shoes, give them money, and pay their bills. Game recognized game and Juicy wasn't going. Yeah he had bought a few pairs of gym shoes, tricked every now and then, but he wasn't any bitches' piggy bank. He had dreams.

Thinking she had offended Juicy Jaleesa said, "Alright lets go post up somewhere but not behind closed doors. Niggas around here to nosy and I don't want my so called business in the street. Let's go on the Place and post up on Booman's porch."

The Place Jaleesa was referring to was right around the corner from Tasha's house off Michigan Avenue and 113th Place, not to be confused with 113th Street. The Southside of Chicago's numbered streets alternated between place and street. For example if you take Michigan Avenue south, toward the Gardens, you passed 113th Street, the 113th Place, the 112th street, then place and so on. It was directly on the next block, if you cut through the alley and a gangway you would be there. As soon as Juicy and Jaleesa hit the block, they saw Booman's porch was empty from the unusual crowd of niggas that hung on the block.

This was Blackstone territory, or the Mo's as they were known for short, a well-known gang that was thick on Chicago's Southside. If you crossed the tracks on 114th, the Gangsta Disciples, or GD's would be at your neck if you were riding under the 5. Many niggas had been shot crossing those tracks on foot for whatever reason. Shit some of the Mo's lived in that territory and had no choice, they understood the need for a hammer.

As Jaleesa grabbed the only available chair on the porch, Juicy went to the gangway to grab some milk crates to sit on.

"I thought this porch would be almost full by now." Jaleesa commented. "I wonder where Booman black ass at, it's even late for him to be waking up."

To Jaleesa the day was almost gone, to these hood niggas, and it was just beginning. Most of them had woken up a few hours ago or were just getting up. That's what happens when your ass stays up all night hustling, drinking and getting high.

"I bet as soon as we flame this blunt he gonna come outside." Juicy said shaking his head.

He knew Booman's ass too well. He had once seen this man wake up in a hospital after three days from a bad reaction to some X, and ask did one of the nigga bring some weed with them.

"I should at least knock on his window, and ask do he want to hit the blunt." Jaleesa said, turning around in her chair to knock on Booman's bedroom window.

"What the fuck?" A voice called out, "I been telling you hypes all night I ain't got shit, its dead till you see me out on them streets today." He boomed.

Mad his ass didn't even pull back this faded ass sheet to see who it was, Jaleesa continued to knock.

"Man what the fuck!" Booman said snatching the sheet so hard it ripped off the nails holding it in place.

"Man," said Booman upon seeing who was on his porch, "here I come Juice."

"What up Mo?" Said Booman, greeting Juicy with the handshake that was sacred to the Blackstone Nation.

"All's well." Answered Juicy as he ended the handshake. "What up Leesa?" Booman greeted Jaleesa. "Now what brings you niggas knocking at my window? You niggas better have a blunt of some kill, my ass in here feening. I can't buy shit until I recop, and this nigga on some bullshit right now." Booman stated, obviously upset that he had missed a lot of money through the night.

"Nigga quit crying and blow your troubles away." Jaleesa said handing him the blunt.

"This some good as shit Mo, where'd you get this from? It taste like somebody grew this shit inside a watermelon Jolly Rancher." Booman commented on the taste. "This shit fruity like a mug, got my mouth watering and shit."

"My cousin out west be tipping this shit." Juicy replied. "Let him tell it, this shit selling like hotcakes."

"I see why." Jaleesa stated as she hit the blunt.

She had only been in rotation twice and she was already feeling it. She was high already.

"If I could get my hands on some of this shit, I wouldn't have to wait on this fucking bird man to bring my shit." Booman confessed.

"You already know that ain't going. The twins ain't having any of that shit. You already know how that goes." Juicy snickered, referring to the law of the streets that the twins supplied all the drugs.

If they didn't have their hands in the pot, your ass better not either, let alone have the balls to sell it in their territory. Juicy had to look at Booman twice as he saw the gears running in his head. He knew this nigga was trying to find some way to get his hands on some of that shit and flood the land. Juicy wanted no parts of Booman's plan though. He was trying to get out the hood, not die in its gutters.

"Boo, shake that shit out ya head man." Juicy warned.

Booman hit the blunt and smiled. His teeth shining white in contrast to his dark skin.

"Nigga, your thoughts are written all over your face." Juicy said shaking his head.

It was just like Booman's ass to think he can out slick a can of oil. They had fought plenty of niggas as kids together, usually behind some shit Booman did, but he was always ride or die for the Mo's and especially Juicy. He had never crossed him before, so Juicy chose to consider the man a friend. He just hoped Booman chose not to cross the twins, they would be less forgiving.

"Anyway!" Jaleesa cut in to change the subject.

The last thing she wanted to hear was anything about someone trying to snake her uncles. It was her duty as family to let them know. She just hoped Juicy didn't prove to be as opportunistic as Booman's thirsty ass. It could get him hurt, or worse.

"I'm about to hit this corner and see if Tasha has made it home yet. I'll get up with you later Juice. Holler at ya Booman." Jaleesa said passing Juicy the blunt and leaving off the porch.

The conversation was making her uncomfortable and she was ready to bounce.

"You ain't even finished you cup ma." Juicy blurted, wanting to spend whatever time he could in her presence.

"That's alright you and Booman kill that, you paid for it anyway."
She responded, quickly leaving the raggedy porch and making her
way around the corner.

Throughout her short lifetime Jaleesa had seen many niggas try
Raymond and Charles and the only place it got them was the hospital
or the grave. She loved and respected her uncles, and wanted no
parts of anyone trying to get at what was theirs. She just hoped
Booman let that idea go so she wouldn't have to hear about them
finding that nigga stinking in the alley. She really hoped Juicy wasn't
crazy enough to fall for it.

It had been about an hour since she and Juicy had gone off to
smoke, so Jaleesa made her way back to Tasha's house hoping she
had made it home. Jaleesa liked to kick it on the block, but without
her girls around the shit was dead. As soon as she made her way
through the gangway, she saw Tasha going in the house with her
arms full of designer bags.

"T", Jaleesa called out from across the street, "where your
baldhead ass been?" Jaleesa joked.

"You and yo momma wish I was baldhead." Tasha shot back,
making sure to flip her natural, silky jet black hair that landed in the
middle of her back. The beautiful texture of hair was compliments of
her Dominican grandmother.

"Where you been girl?"

"Mako took me out to lunch and we did a little shopping."

"Little? Looks like you bought out Macy's and Ann Klein to me."
Jaleesa remarked, as she helped Tasha with some of her bags.

"These niggas know they got to pay to play, and I play big girl
games. Ya feel me?"

"Tasha you're is ass crazy."

Jaleesa began to break down a Vega and roll some of that weed up Juicy had. Grabbing a glamour magazine, Jaleesa began to break down the weed that came in a little seal with blue sharks on it.

Before she could open the bag good Tasha exclaimed, "Girl where you get that shit from?"

Tasha was admiring the almost neon blue and violet hairs that ran through the light green buds.

"You went to the buildings on the low end to get this? I might have to buy that nigga out that got this shit." Tasha said picking up the magazine and examining the weed more closely.

"Girl I got this shit from Juice. Ain't it disrespectful and loud as hell?" Jaleesa said, commenting on the strong smell emanating from the little sack.

"Juice plugged like that?" Tasha inquired. "I knew the nigga sold a few bags here and there but Juicy done come the fuck up."

"Shit!" Jaleesa exclaimed," this blunt cracked like a mug. Ain't no way I can band aid it, you got an empty?" She asked Tasha.

"No you gotta go to Zach's boo."

"Why I gotta go?"

"Cause I got to piss like a mug and you ain't doing shit else." Tasha said running towards the bathroom and closing the door.

Shit! Jaleesa thought, *I just came from this mofo store.* Slipping her sandals back on her feet and locking the door she went to Zach's.

****

81

"Mako ya girl left a bag in the backseat." Timmo noticed, as they were about to hop on the Dan Ryan and head back out west.

"She can get it later." Mako replied, knowing he had some runs he needed to make.

He thought about what was in that bag, the dress Tasha had planned on wearing to his graduation party. After trying on about twenty outfits, she let him decide on which one he wanted to see her in the most. To be honest Mako didn't care, he wanted to see Tasha without anything on, but he knew that wasn't going to happen any time soon, so he would settle for imagining tearing the dress he'd chosen off of her.

"Let me turn around and drop this off, she is gonna have a fit when she realize it's not there." Mako said busting an illegal U-turn and heading back up the hill.

The dress that he had chosen for her was a beautiful, princess waist, pastel print, Anne Klein, summer dress. He wanted her to look perfect because she would be meeting his grandfather, and Mako knew what a critical eye he had. Abraham would be observing everything, from what she wore, to what perfume she wore, how well her manicure was, and did she possess the proper etiquette of a lady. If Mako was to have an official girlfriend, she had to enhance the family image not bring it down.

Jaleesa was stepping out of the store when she saw a familiar car pull up in front of Zach's. No one else around there drove a smoke grey, custom painted E-class with custom titanium rims, and pitch black tinted windows, but her Uncle Raymond. The quality of the Bose speakers were impressive as they flooded the block with music so clear, you'd have thought Rick Ross was shooting a video on the Avenue.

"Hey, how's my favourite niece?" Raymond said rolling down the passenger side car window. "Where are you headed, to mi casa?"

82

"Aw Uncle Raymond, why you even asking silly questions." Jaleesa joked as she hopped into the passenger seat. The soft cool leather felt good to her skin and she sunk back for the short ride.

"So how've you been doing, I haven't seen you in a while?"

"I'm good, just trying to get my money right, so I can start college this fall, and have as much fun as possible this summer."

"College? Why is this my first time hearing about this?" Raymond said surprised. "I didn't think that was on your agenda, Niece."

"It wasn't at first, to be honest, but I don't want to work these funky minimum wage jobs all my life. I'm actually thinking about owning my own day care one day in the hood. Somebody got to teach these little heathens right." Jaleesa laughed.

"I know that's right!" Raymond joined in.

Deep down inside, Raymond was very proud of Jaleesa for deciding to go to school. He knew the only thing these streets had to offer was pain and heartache, he believed both of his nieces, Tasha and Jaleesa deserved more. Tasha's problem was she was spoiled rotten and saw no need to accumulate any wealth on her own. She always knew she would be taken care of. Jaleesa on the other hand was being raised by a single mother, who refused any financial help from her father because of the lifestyle he chose to live. Jaleesa didn't suffer however, if anything it made her a stronger, independent woman, who had a small taste of struggle and decided it wasn't her taste.

"Thanks for the ride Uncle Raymond." Jaleesa chirped, opening the passenger door.

"Wait a second niece, I have something for you", Raymond said, before letting Jaleesa out in front of a place he once called home, but now rarely visited.

He reached into his pockets and peeled off twenty crisp one hundred dollar bills and handed them to Jaleesa.

"Whoa Uncle!" Jaleesa exclaimed. "You don't have to give me this, I'm straight." Jaleesa uttered, feeling uncomfortable about taking such a large sum of money from him.

He had always given Jaleesa a few ends here and there, especially if Tasha was around when he was dishing out loot, but she never would have expected this much, let alone asked for it.

"Here, take it." Raymond said, firmly pressing the money into Jaleesa hands "This is going to help you buy those books for school okay?"

As Jaleesa put the money in her pocket and got out of the car, she was startled by a horn honking loudly behind her.

"What the fuck?" She yelled, only to turn around and see Mako smiling through the front window gesturing for her to come over.

What this nigga want, she thought. "Probably looking for Tasha.

"Hey ma, what's up?" Mako greeted Jaleesa.

"Hey what's up?"

"Your girl left her bag in my car, do me a favour and run it upstairs to her. I know that's where you're on your way to."

"Don't assume to know where I am on my way to." Jaleesa snapped. "But I'll give it to her."

Mako was cool and all, but there was something about him Jaleesa just didn't like. He seemed too slick for her, but if Tasha liked it, she loved it. She knew this was exactly her girl's type of guy and

84

she wished them all the best. Before Jaleesa could make it to the porch Timmo asked her a question.

"Aye that ride you just hopped out of, that paint job and system is tight as hell. That your guy's car?" He inquired.

Sensing Jaleesa was about to cuss him out for getting in her business Timmo quickly added, "I was just wondering where he got that paint job done."

"First of all nosy ass, that ain't my guy's car, I don't have a guy. Second of all that is my uncle's ride and I don't know where he got all that shit done." Jaleesa spat. "Are we through here?"

"Damn ma, a nigga can't ask a question?"

"No he can't." Jaleesa sneered, walking in the house and closing the door.

"What was that all about?" Mako asked Timmo.

"Man yo ass don't know shit do you? It's only one nigga in this whole city who got a ride like that. I just wanted to confirm some information."

"Okay nigga what is you talking about, I'm confused as hell right now?"

"Her uncle is none other than Raymond Johnson, the brains behind the infamous Southside twins."

"Get the fuck out of here! You have got to be kidding me!"

Mako really didn't know how to digest this information. He had been trying for the longest to branch out and make new moves. College was over, and he wasn't quite ready to sit behind a desk and kiss political ass all day. No, he wanted to get as rich as he could off the game. He wanted his name to ring in the streets, like his father's once did. The kind of respect Mako wanted couldn't be found in corporate America, it could only be found in the streets.

To Mako, this was a sign that the gods were shining down in his favour. It was meant for him to get a piece of the pie out south. With his girl's best friend being plugged with the twins, he could pump Tasha for info to see what the word on the street was and find a way to make some money off of it. Tasha was cool and all, but he liked money more. It was as if opportunity just knocked, and Mako was determined to answer the door.

CHAPTER 7

Get In Where You Fit In

Summer was quickly flying by. Mako had introduced Tasha to his grandfather at the graduation party, and he seemed to be pleased with his choice of woman. In the meantime however, Mako was busy putting a plan together so that he could start pushing some product out south. Roseland was going to be his test sight. He knew that the twins had some excellent connects when it came to dope, but Mako had found one who's product could be stepped on numerous times. He had come up with the perfect plan; he just was having trouble finding someone out there willing to sell his product.

Mako and Timmo were posted up at Timmo's tip on the west side in a neighbourhood known as the Village. The Village consisted of housing projects that included high rises as well as row houses. Timmo resided in one of the high rises in the Jane Adams complex. The complex had been slated for demolition within the next few months, with the city offering the residents either Section 8 to relocate, relocation to another housing project on the city Southside, or the opportunity to stay in the Village and move into one of the newly rehabbed row houses.

You would think that people actually wanted an opportunity to live in a better neighbourhood with better schools, and opportunities for their children, but you would be wrong. When rumours of the buildings being torn down started to float, the residents were upset and many didn't want to move. This was their home, no matter how decrepit, unsafe, and fucked up it was, it was theirs and they didn't like having to leave it.

With the city's relocation plans, a few things were certain to happen, gang rivalries, turf wars, and murders would be on the rise. The Southside and Westside people didn't get along, somehow believing one hood was better than the other, not being able to see the squalor they all lived in. Knowing his family might soon have to move from the place that nurtured his black, greedy heart Timmo knew that he was going have to find a way to eat no matter where he went. Mako constantly in his ear trying to convince him to take the Section 8 and move to Roseland to lock it down was starting to sound better every day.

"Alright man, so your cousin Juicy stays out that way?" Mako asked Timmo.

"Yeah man, a few blocks down from your girl Tasha, but I keep telling you man, he in good with the twins and he ain't gonna push your shit willingly in the hood." Timmo barked for the third time.

"That's not what I need him for. If that nigga is as plugged as you say, he is gonna be your ears to the streets. Get in good with the nigga, find out who in his crew ain't happy with the way things are working out there. Cause a little descent, you know divide and conquer." Mako instructed.

Timmo had to laugh, "Man that shit is a lot easier said than done. The twins got eyes and ears everywhere, you either get down with them, or don't get down at all."

"Well what about your girl Kristen?"

"What about her?" Timmo and Kristen had been out a few times and she showed him that her pussy and that bomb ass head was worth every dollar he had contributed since that day. He wasn't territorial about no bitches, but he could see the gears grinding in Mako's head as he was sure to come up with some scheme. Timmo tried to stop those gears right in there tracks.

"Listen man, I feel ya but have you even run this idea by your grandfather yet? You know he told your ass to stay out these streets, especially with election season coming up. I don't think he's going to take too kindly to you disobeying him."

Timmo knew that he was not a favorite of Abraham. Abraham often blamed his relationship with Mako for the trouble Mako got into. What Abraham didn't understand was Mako was the brains, and Timmo was just the man behind the scenes with the resources. It was Mako's idea for the college drug ring, all Timmo did was supply the connect that would be out of the range of his grandfather's prying eyes.

"So what's the plan?" Timmo asked, while ashing a fat blunt of some diesel. "I can tell your mind has some get rich quick, before your Pops finds out, scheme in that thick ass head of yours." Timmo laughed.

Taking the blunt from Timmo's outstretched hand and hitting it Mako responded.

"This is what I'm thinking about, this flame ass shit right here. We the only niggas out west with this high quality shit. There is no reason for us not to share it with our neighbours to the south."

Mako had been thinking on how he would pursue his lucrative drug endeavour in Roseland. He didn't really have any connections out there other than Timmo's cousin Juicy, who had already copped some of the weed from him earlier that week. That nigga said it wasn't shit like that on his end of town and niggas would go crazy for it. Mako was ready to test that theory.

"Peep game T, you are gonna give up your apartment out here and take that Section 8."

Before Timmo could object, Mako silenced him with the wave of his hand.

"In order for us to progress, we gotta leave the Village behind and head out south. The easiest way to set up shop is to live out there."

"It's almost like divine intervention that you got the opportunity to get Section 8. Take it, get a crib in the Hundreds, not in Roseland but close enough and then we are going to test the waters with this gristle we got and move from there."

Timmo like the idea Mako had but, he was not planning on ever leaving the Village. This was his home, where he came of age in the streets. All his memories could be found in this ten block radius of high rise buildings, drugs dealers, thugs, fiends and fatherless children. Hell, he was one of those fatherless children.

The ABLA Community Centre on Loomis is where he had his first fight. Timmo would never forget how he was ready to fight to the death over the only thing his father ever gave him, other than life; his first pair of Mikes. For some reason two teenagers thought a scrawny, big foot, 11 year old was giving up those shoes without a fight. By the time the fight was over, he was bloody and bruised, his Mike's were a little scuffed up but he walked away with them on his feet, and his baby manhood intact.

"Nigga is you hearing me?" Mako said, snapping Timmo out of his thoughts.

"Man I don't know about leaving the Village, this is my home, everything I know is here and above all this is where I get money my man." Timmo said trying to fight the inevitable tide that was coming.

Whether he left on Mako's accord or not, the city was tearing down the buildings and relocating its residence. He was going to have to leave eventually, but he thought it would be later, rather than sooner.

"How you gonna make money in a place that will no longer exist in the next eighteen months?" Mako questioned. "I know it's hard, but it's time to move on my nigga. We need to get in where we fit in, and we will fit just perfectly out south."

For the next two hours over Hennessey and chronic, Mako discussed his plan with Timmo. They disagreed on the best way to go about handling their business without tipping the twins off too quick. They planned on pushing some of the chronic through the neighbourhood, with a plan to eventually get in on the dope sales out there. Whereas the Westside had an overwhelming abundance of heroin users, the Southside was full of crack heads. There were a few spots out south that sold heroin, but their hypes blew the spot up so fast, it was almost impossible to keep it in business for longer than a few months before the CPD rolled through.

Mako decided that it was in his best interest to invest in the heroin. That way, he could get his money right fast and let his product do the talking. One thing about fiends, they didn't have loyalty to any one dealer or supplier. Whoever had the fattest bags and the best dope got their crumpled up dollars. Mako would need every single one of those crumpled up dollars to fund his illegal enterprise. His grandfather may have had dreams of being the mayor, but Mako had dreams of running the city, just as his father before him had back in the day. Mako wanted to honor his father by showing Abraham that he was worthy of running the family business, in the streets as well as the boardroom. There were two sides to the Clark family legacy, the one the public saw that portrayed Abraham as a handsome charismatic politician in the limelight, but only those who truly knew him knew all his political campaigns and those he endorsed with large checks were fuelled with dope money.

Although Mako had told Timmo he needed to get in where he fit in, he wasn't all that sure where he fit in himself. On one hand he was a handsome, intelligent, articulate, middle class black man, with a degree in business management. He could excel in any profession he decided to choose. On the other side of the coin, he came from a line of calculating, ruthless hustlers. Men who worked their way up in the ranks and offered their offspring a better existence than the one given to them, but all in all, they were gangsters. They bred hustlers and demanded loyalty at all cost.

91

He couldn't understand how his grandfather expected him to be something other than what he was born to be. This was Mako's last summer to be the wild child his grandfather had always known. It was also time for him to decide where he fit in exactly, did he want to be in the streets or in corporate America. He loved being recognized and praised in the hood. The attention a ghetto superstar received had no equal in his eyes. Yet, at the same time he knew it was his grandfather's political connections that kept his illegal enterprises well hidden.

Abraham had elevated his game over the years from selling drugs, to selling bids for city contracts. He went from ducking police to attending the police commissioners intimate 60th birthday party. He no longer collected profits from the drug game. Abraham wisely decided to give that part of his empire to Macon Sr.'s best friend Terry. Over the years he had showed his loyalty to the family and Abraham rewarded him with a very lucrative drug empire, with only one string attached, he had to go through the supplier Abraham had used for over twenty years. Other than that, the profits were his and Terry came out on top.

This summer Mako had decided would be his defining moment, either he rose to the top like cream, or sunk to the bottom with the rest of the dregs. The stakes were very high for him, if he failed, or got caught up in his scheme, his grandfather and everything he worked for would feel the repercussion of Mako's decision, but he was smart, or so he thought. Smart enough to not get his hands directly into the pot that is what he had his roadie Timmo for. Timmo got down how he lived and would lay cats to rest if his money was on the line. The two of them could conquer the city, with Mako behind the scenes. Mako liked the thought of that.

"So, what's up T? are you going to put in this bid for Section 8 so we can get it cracking or what?"

When Timmo looked at Mako, he knew his man's mind was made up so he finally relented and filled out the paper work.

92

"Nigga this shit better work," Timmo warned, "cause if it doesn't the only place either of us will fit is gonna be a cell or a coffin."

Three weeks later Timmo's Section 8 was approved, two weeks later he found a crib on the corner of 109th and Indiana. From then on it was only a matter of time before they would get things popping in Roseland.

CHAPTER 8

A Familiar Face

Mako decided to throw Timmo a major going away blow out in one of the buildings in K town his grandfather owned. The building was located on 14th and Kostner and had been in his family long before he was born. During his junior year Mako had convinced his grandfather to allow him to turn one of the second floor apartments into an apartment for himself, under the premise that it was a closer drive to the university than it had been coming from the suburbs. At first Abraham was adamant about his grandson living in such a poor and violent neighbourhood, despite the fact that he had grown up there in a time where it was still decent. Abraham also knew his grandson had to be up to something wanting to move from their luxurious five thousand square foot home into an apartment in the center of one of Chicago's worst ghettos. Abraham still owned a few buildings in the neighbourhood and made sure that he kept them clean as possible and running efficiently enough to satisfy Section 8 standards. The particular building Mako was trying to move in had fortunately been kept up more than the others, it was special to his grandfather so he preserved the building to preserve the memories made there.

It took months of cajoling on Mako's part. He finally won with arguments that would appeal to the politician in his grandfather. "Pops, just think about it, how many politicians represent districts they wouldn't dare live in? You would be showing the voters that not only do you work in that district, you live there also, in a way." Seeing something click in his grandfather's mind he went on. "With all this talk about re-gentrification and restoring our neighbourhoods to their former glory, it will not only line your pockets but the ballot boxes as well. Besides, everyone in that neighbourhood knows who you are and who I am, you don't have to fear for my safety. I'm over there all the time anyway."

"And that's the problem Macon, too many of the wrong people know who you are and you have a way of attracting the dregs of society, which by the way are all that live in that area."

"Pops, you are from that area and you are definitely the cream. I'm a man and I can handle my own, we all have to make our own way. I can't live in your home forever, and I am definitely not doing the dorms."

Two weeks later Abraham began renovating the apartment building on Kostner and a few other properties in the area.

＊＊＊＊＊＊＊＊＊＊＊＊＊

Jaleesa, Tasha and Kristen had decided to meet up at Tasha's house to get dressed and pre-party before they made their way out west to Timmo's Moving South Bash.

"I really hate kicking it out west." Jaleesa griped. "Those cats grimy as hell and you know they love to rob people. I ain't trying to get stuck up tonight."

"And we're going to K-town, T you must be in love with this nigga." Kristen laughed.

"Let me let you girls in on a little secret." Tasha said adjusting her bra for maximum cleavage in her Roberto Cavalli sheer tank top. "Truth be told, west side niggas are the real ballers in the city. Now don't get me wrong some of them are out south, but the true go getters live out west."

"Well thank you for the lesson on ghetto niggas and where to find the richest one." Jaleesa quipped, rolling her eyes.

She loved Tasha, but sometimes she could be so shallow and materialistic it bugged the hell out of her. The girl already had everything, what more could she possibly want? Jaleesa had remembered when her Aunt Jackie died and had seen how quick her mother fled the ghetto afterward. She was raised to know this was not the type of life for anyone to live. No matter how your life ended, in the ghetto the circumstances were usually violent or avoidable. She didn't want to be another casualty, so she tried to steer clear of hood dudes. That's probably why she had never let anyone partake of her pleasure. Regardless, this was her last year kicking it on the block. When the fall came, it would be deuces to the hood and all it represented, she was going to college.

An hour later the three girls pulled up in front of Mako's building and were mildly surprised. On the outside the building didn't look to welcoming due to the scaffolding in front that was left up by the construction workers as they repaired the buildings outside, and there were a few dope fiends lingering in the gangway.

"Are you sure this is the right building?" Jaleesa asked.

"Yes it is, 1416, and can't you hear the music coming from inside? This must be the place." Tasha answered. "Now make sure all valuables are out of plain sight, because if someone bust my uncle's window for your shit, I don't want to hear his mouth."

When the girls were buzzed in at the front door, their senses were assaulted with the smell of good weed, expensive alcohol, and loud rap music. The house was packed with people gambling, drinking, smoking, and basically having a good time. Tasha wasn't really into house parties in anyone else's hood, but she trusted that Mako would let no harm come to her.

"Do you see the inside of this mofo?" Kristen said in awe as she took in the renovated three bedroom apartment.

They all had been in hundreds of old apartment buildings in the city that had been renovated, which usually consisted of a fresh coat of paint and cheap carpeting, but this had been restored to its original beauty and beyond.

Jaleesa couldn't believe this was the same questionably raggedy building she had stepped into just moments before as she stared at the shine on the restored hardwood floors. With flat screen TV's in all the rooms, including the bathroom, Jaleesa realized Mako was making some serious dough that probably came from some type of illegal activity. The only time she saw any luxuries close to what Mako's apartment had were when she went to visit Tasha, but even this place had a leg up on Tasha's building.

"Damn T, you made a come up!" Kristen yelped with an undetectable trace of envy.

"I told you lames I knew a baller when I saw one, and here he comes right now." Tasha smirked.

Mako stepped away from the dice game when he saw Tasha and her girls come into the room where people were gambling. Pitty Pat, Spades, and dice were the choice for tonight's betters and there was big money on the table.

"Hey ma, I'm happy to see you made it in one piece." Mako joked, as he embraced Tasha. "Go grab you something to drink out the kitchen and let me finish taking these dudes' money."

"Well let's get it in!" Kristen yelled, before Tasha could respond. "Where's Tim?"

They had fucked a few times and she decided she was going to stay in his pockets as long as she could. When they were together he got her whatever she asked for and treated her respectfully, for the most part. Regardless, it was more than any other man she had opened her legs for had done, and she was really starting to fall for him.

"I'm not sure, probably in the back smoking up Peru." Mako joked.

97

Literally every square inch of surface area in the kitchen was covered with bottles of liquor. Whether you could name it or not, they had it. Mako had even sprung for a few cases of Angel, which is the world's most expensive champagne, coming in at $2200 per bottle. It was as if his kitchen doubled as a high end liquor store.

"Ooohh!" Tasha squealed, as she saw the unopened case of Angel. "I can't believe these ghetto people passed up this for the Crystal and DP. Compared to this champagne that shit is like drinking a bud light. A toast to better things and bigger ballers.

"This shit is disgusting." Kristen said, making a face at the cup of champagne. "I'll stick to the ghetto shit like Remy and Hennessey."

"I'm with Kristen on that." Jaleesa said. "This tastes like vinegar."

Tasha rolled her eyes. "I guess you can't buy taste." She joked with the girls.

At that moment Mako came up behind her and kissed the back of her neck.

"I located Tim for you Kristen. He is on the back porch in his studio laying down some tracks, out the kitchen door and to the left."

"Thanks Mako, I'll catch you girls later." Kristen giggled as she disappeared out the back door.

"Jaleesa, you look like you need a drink." Mako commented, seeing Jaleesa appeared to be uncomfortable.

He had something to show Tasha and he knew she wouldn't leave her girl alone if she was uncomfortable.

"I'm good," she responded, "I'm just taking in my surroundings." Jaleesa convincingly responded.

She sensed that Mako wanted to be alone with Tasha, and encouraged them to go and enjoy themselves. Before walking away Mako gave Jaleesa a quarter ounce of some buds he called Juicy Fruit.

"I remember you ain't smoking if you ain't rolling." He said, throwing her a playful wink before taking Tasha away.

"Good looking." She mumbled under her breath, as she looked at the bag of bud he had given her.

It looked familiar and smelled just like that blunt she had smoked with Juicy. That bud was really distinctive and since that day she hadn't found anything that even came close.

Jaleesa went out on the back porch with the rest of the weed smokers. There was fifteen to twenty people out there congregating, laughing, and smoking, but she finally managed to find a milk crate to sit on. She needed to roll without having to spend another minute teetering on those five inch stilettos. She went to reach for her purse and remembered she had left it under the seat in the truck, now she had to ask one of the dudes for a blunt.

She dreaded having to start a conversation with anyone out there, she didn't want someone thinking she was trying to flirt because she wasn't even on that. She was just trying to be on this good. Not wanting to lose her crate, she tapped the back nearest to her and said excuse me. When the guy turned around she was shocked to see Juicy's face.

"What're you doing out here?" They both questioned at the same time, getting a good laugh about the timing.

Jaleesa explained to him how Tasha was messing with Mako and inquired on who he knew there.

"It's my cousin Tim's party, and that Kush you smoking is his too. That's the same shit we smoked with Booman that day."

After handing Jaleesa an empty, they began making small talk. Jaleesa instantly relaxed seeing a familiar face in the crowd and decided she would stick close to Juicy until she could catch up with the rest of the crew that night. She just hoped she wasn't cock blocking.

Juicy couldn't help but to stare at Jaleesa while she licked and rolled the blunt. He was seriously into her, but knew she wasn't on the same page. He had always thought she was pretty, but today with those skin tight leggings, and the fuchsia Fendi halter top, she was looking gorgeous. That coupled with the fact that he was feeling buzzed caused his dick to jump.

"Juicy, are you listening to me?" Jaleesa asked.

"Yeah I'm looking, I mean listening you."

Jaleesa looked up at him and gave him a little smirk.

"Well what did I just say?"

"I was doing more looking than listening, I'll admit, but when you get dressed up Leesa you are bad as hell! You already know that though." He said quickly, taking a swig from his cup to stop himself from tasting his shoe again.

"Thanks Juice." Jaleesa said bashfully.

She didn't like Juicy like that, so why was his compliment giving her butterflies. She flamed up the blunt and they smoked in silence. Every now and then someone would come and speak to Juicy, most wanting to know was that him, referring to her. After one to many dudes tried to holler at her, she told Juicy to claim her to the next person that asked.

"You know I don't do street niggas Juice and when you say no, they can be ignorant as hell and I am not trying to be called either a

100

stuck up bitch, or having to fight tonight. So for everyone's enjoyment, just go with it."

Juicy had to laugh at that. He always wanted to be able to call Jaleesa his girl, and even if this was for show, he would play his part to the fullest. So after getting tired of sitting on the milk crate they went inside to see if they could find better seating for her, and a bathroom for him. After squeezing onto one of the couches between a half sleep drunk chick, and a girl with a pair of shorts that looked like blue jean panties, she checked her phone to see what time it was. She knew it was late because the crowd had begun to thin, but there was still a lot of people there, the ones who refused to leave until the last drop was drank, or the last blunt smoked. Shit is was almost three in the morning and they were nowhere near finishing the liquor or the weed. Jaleesa was done. She wanted she wanted some breakfast and that nice warm bed at Tasha's house any minute.

When Juicy came out the bathroom, drying his hands on his pants she had to smile. What hood dude washes his hands after he uses the bathroom? Juicy did.

"You look like you're done for the night Leesa, you ready to go back out South? I can give you a ride home."

"Let me hit Tasha's phone. I haven't seen that chick since we got here. Mako's got her somewhere hemmed up." She said playfully, speed dialling Tasha.

After calling three times and being sent directly to voicemail, she received two texts. One from Tasha telling her she was spending the night with Mako and she could take the truck whenever she was ready to leave, but not to leave Kristen. Tasha emphasized that, knowing Jaleesa wouldn't bother to look for her on her way out the door. The next text was from Kristen saying she was not coming home tonight, and to pass the word to Tasha because she wasn't answering the phone or text.

"Well that's my cue." Jaleesa said, texting Tasha back that Kristen was straight and she was riding home with Juicy.

Tasha text back adding that she would see her in the morning.

"Okay Juice, let's roll." Jaleesa said, standing up and realizing she wasn't going to make it one more minute with those damn shoes on.

"You wanna go to the truck stop on Pershing?" Juicy asked once they were in the car.

"Most definitely, I can taste the steak and pancakes right now." She said as her stomach grumbled at the thought.

Juicy had turned the music up so that he wouldn't have to make awkward conversation with her. He really dug Jaleesa and didn't want to embarrass himself by saying the wrong thing. He knew he would never be her type, she didn't talk to dudes from the neighbourhood. He couldn't really blame her, they weren't on shit, but he was different, He went to school and was about to graduate at the top of his class, although that wasn't saying much for a community college, but he tried. He knew he wasn't going to live in the ghetto forever.

By the time they pulled up at the truck stop, Jaleesa was trying to keep her eyes open, but as soon as she smelled the food she was unlocking the car door.

"I've never seen someone wake up that fast." Juicy laughed.

"I wasn't sleep, I was just resting my eyes." She pouted playfully, getting out the car.

On the way home, Jaleesa was sleep by the time they hit 79th. Juicy was happy the highway was clear at this time of morning because he couldn't stop himself from glancing over catching stares of Jaleesa while she slept. She looked so peaceful and perfect, serene even. The soft snore she emitted made him chuckle, he knew if he said something she would never admit to snoring on the ride home. Pulling up in front of Tasha's building, Juicy stared at her one last time trying to burn the image of her beauty sleep in his memory before waking her up.

"Leesa, we're here ma." He whispered, gently shaking her awake.

"Hmmm, oh alright, thanks for the ride Juice." She whimpered groggily as she got out of his car and fumbled for Tasha's house keys in her purse.

Juicy waited for her to get in the house, and gave her time to lock the doors before he drove himself home.

One day, he thought, *one day Sleeping Beauty, I will be worthy to be your prince.*

CHAPTER 9

Southside

"Man I hate living out here." Timmo gripped for the one hundredth time since he had moved to the south side.

He had only been living there for three weeks and found any and everything to complain about. Today it was because he couldn't find a decent Italian Beef to eat anywhere close by.

"Man gas high as hell and I got to drive all the ways to Domenzo's for a decent Italian Beef. These out south niggas ain't good for shit." He cursed, as he sat at the kitchen table bagging up some hydro.

Mako laughed as he tossed a greasy bag that contained an Italian beef and some fries on the table.

"For you bro and all that you do." Mako chuckled.

"Hell yeah man, good looking out." Timmo said grabbing the bag of food.

Mako watched him eat half the sandwich in three bites, after eating a mouthful of fries Tim told Mako how business was going in Roseland.

"Getting in was easier than I thought. My cousin Juicy lives out here and he introduced to me to a few cats. I blew a few blunts with some of them and threw out a hook, but no one was biting. The twins got these niggas spooked." He explained, taking another large bite of his sandwich.

"So are you gonna finish talking or make love to the food man." Mako urged his friend to keep speaking.

"Damn can't a nigga eat?" Tim asked wiping juice from his chin. Setting the sandwich down, he picked up where he left off. "Anyway, like I said these niggas was acting real scary like they didn't want no action until Juicy introduced me to one of the Moe's out here, Booman."

Timmo looked at his sandwich like he was going to take another bite, but the look on Mako's face stopped him. Knowing he wasn't going to enjoy his sandwich until he was through, he wiped his hands on a napkin and finished.

"Booman approached me a few days later at the liquor store down the hill, letting me know that there was not too many dudes out here willing to risk pushing anything unless the twins branded it, but he was more than ready and willing."

Tim went on to explain how he had given Booman a QP to sell and in less than three hours he was hitting his hip, letting him know the shit was going like hotcakes.

"Here's the catch 22 though," Timmo began, "he claims he can't sell anything larger than a QP without the twins finding out about it. I told him I wasn't about no nickel and dime selling, that I was trying to push weight. He told me to give him a day to work around the problem and he would hit me back."

"Is that it?" Mako questioned, assuming there was more to the story.

"Yea that's it nigga." Timmo said finishing off the rest of his meal. "Booman should be hitting me any minute."

As if on cue, Timmo's phone began to vibrate. Looking at the caller ID and giving Mako a look, Timmo answered it. After a few one worded replies Timmo let Mako know Booman was on his way.

"Alright bro I'm out." Mako said, giving dap to his buddy.

"Why are you leaving so soon, you just got here?" Timmo inquired.

"Timmo, as long as you out here grinding, I cannot be seen with you like that my man. When we move on to the next level and the money starts flowing, people are going to put two and two together. For the sake of business we can't let that happen."

"Oh, so you brought me out here just to abandon me in the wild bro?" Timmo asked, feeling slighted.

"It's not like that. You get out here and make this money and when we get together it always has to be out west. I don't want any of the twins' eyes on me. Can't you understand that?"

Relenting, Timmo accepted the terms of this money making scheme and decided Mako was right. He could admit his friend had more in the brains department, but he knew he was the muscle and the real money maker in this partnership. Mako just had the crazy schemes that helped Timmo accomplish his hood dreams, but what if his dreams were bigger than the hood? Just as he was about to delve deeper into that thought his doorbell rang.

This little sneaky mofo, Tim thought as Booman gave him the full scope of the neighborhood, its suppliers and inconsistencies the twins watched for constantly. Booman let Timmo know that from 112th and Michigan all the way to 115th and Michigan the twins owned 90% of the stores, which they leased to anyone from the Asians to the Arabs, to regular guys from the hood, who sold whatever out of their stores as a mask to illegal activities.

"Over east?" Tim questioned. "I'm trying to get my grind on out south, where the hell did the east side come in?"

"The twins presence can be felt over east too, but they don't have stomping grounds out there. They push their weight through some cat named C-low." Booman explained. "If we can cut in on that action in South Shore, we can still put a dent in their pockets and it would lay the ground work for us to get on in Roseland."

Booman could see that Timmo was not really going for his plan.

"Look, the twins have eyes and ears everywhere in Roseland. They know their product, and keep track of everyone who sells it, and how much they sell." Booman continued. He also added that it only applied to people who bought larger quantities. "So if you want to push weight, we need to test the waters and start over east. That way, not only will you get a larger customer base, but you will have a backdoor to the twins' empire out south. You don't have to test the waters with weed, you can hit the streets with some of that butter."

Timmo pondered this suggestion as he rolled up a blunt from his personal stash. He knew that Mako was ready to flood the Roseland area with his product, but as of now the safest thing to sell was hydro, until they could find a way around the twins. It was lucrative, but not as lucrative as the crack or heroin business.

"So I take it you know some cats over east willing to get down, I take it?" He asked, handing Booman the spliff.

"I got a few people in mind, who C-Low decided couldn't eat over east anymore that are on standby, ready to get this paper."

Timmo couldn't help but to wonder how this dude had connects of some kind all over the city, but didn't have the bread to show for it. That was a red flag for him, this little nigga couldn't really be trusted and before deciding to agree with his plan, Timmo made a mental note to keep a close eye on this dude.

"Alright my man, tell me what you need so we can get it cracking on the Shore."

Before Booman left, Timmo had hit his hand with a half a bird of cola and gave him one week to return his profit.

"Booman, just a word of advice. I don't play with my money." He warned before shutting his door.

CHAPTER 10

Down on the Shore

As soon as Timmo gave Booman the product, he hopped in a cab and was on his way to his baby momma's house on 73rd and Jefferies. He wasn't sure if he would be welcomed or not. He hadn't seen his two year old son in about five months. His trifling ass hadn't dropped off any money, not even a phone call to see if his namesake was still breathing. He knew the first thing he would have to do is hit Kareema's hand. He wasn't worried about that though, since he had been making money off the twins and Timmo. He had a few extra scraps to throw her. Hell the fifteen hundred he had put up for her was more than scraps, but it was part of his plan since the day he decided starting over east was the best option.

At the last minute, he decided to have the cab driver stop at the liquor store. He decided not only was this cause for a celebration for him, but the Remy would definitely make his baby momma more pliable. Hell, Remy is how she ended up being his baby momma after all. He had to tell the cab driver to slow down as they turned on to Kareema's block. Like many hood niggas, he never learned the address to a building, just what it looked like and what it was close to.

Kareema's building was catty corner to a large Catholic church that had seen better days when South Shore was once filled with prosperous white people. The large apartment buildings and two and three flats were still in fairly decent condition. During daylight hours it gave unknowing passer byers a sense of serenity, but everyone in this area knew when the street lights came on, the dealers, fiends and killers would be out in full force.

When he got to the courtyard, Booman had the hardest time trying to remember which bell was hers, but didn't worry about getting in the gate as he saw an old lady with grocery bags approaching. He went in the gate behind her and entered the courtyard. He was hesitant to ring the bell that had Kareema's apartment number. What if she wouldn't let him in? What if she wasn't home? What if she didn't live there anymore? He figured he would soon find out.

When Booman got up the three flights of stairs he found that the front door was slightly ajar to let him in. He was thinking how unsafe, she hadn't even asked who was at the door. Sitting on the couch was Kareema, looking as high as all get out.

"Well look what the fucking cat dragged in. I hope you came to drop off some cash, or you can leave the way you came in." She spat at Booman.

"I just came by to see my son." Booman said throwing his hands up in surrender.

"Ha!" Kareema laughed scornfully. "What makes today so much more special than the last six months?"

"Well I can leave if you want me to." Booman said, pretending to head for the front door. "But how would our son feel knowing you kept him away from me when I came to see him?"

"Run that game on another bitch! He is only two and who's gonna tell him? Not me."

Just as Kareema was about to dig into Booman's ass on how trifling a father he was, Jason woke up from his nap and came into the living room. Still half asleep, he ran to his father upon realizing he was truly there.

"Daddy, Daddy!" He yelled, with his tiny voice.

"Hey little man!" Booman said, scooping him up inside his arms and holding him up to eye level. They looked so much alike that Booman felt a shiver up his spine. He couldn't believe that he had a mini him walking around. He took his son in for another few seconds in awe and wonder before hugging him again and setting him down. Seeing this as the perfect opportunity to play on Kareema's emotions, he started to the front door.

Seeing his father head toward the nearest exit sent Jason into high pitched wailing and tears.

"No go Daddy, no go!" Jason screamed.

"Shit!" Kareema mumbled.

She was about to let his ass walk out that door until her son looked at her with eyes the most hurtful pleading in his eyes.

"Daddy is not going anywhere baby, he's just putting his bag down." Kareema assured her son, but was throwing daggers at Booman with her eyes.

She knew he was going to leave eventually, she just hoped that this time it would be when Jason was sleeping so she didn't have to lie and soothe her son about his father's latest disappearance.

****

Kareema was surprised. Spending the day with Booman and her son had actually been pleasant. After he had given her some money, he told her to get dressed because he was going to take his son to Chuck E Cheese's. At hearing the word Chuck E., Jason began to squeal in delight and rushed to his room.

"Dress mommy, dress!"

Booman had spent over a hundred dollars in Chuck E. coins and let his son run wild playing games he really didn't understand over and over. Jason stuffed his little face with all the pizza he could. After a few hours of playing, he still wasn't ready to leave, but fell asleep quickly on the train ride home.

When they got in the house, Kareema laid him in his bedroom and closed the door. Booman was flaming up a blunt as she walked from the back of the apartment. He motioned for Kareema to sit next to him on the couch, she hesitated. She knew he was up to something, and hoped he wasn't looking for sexual favors because she was tired of him stopping in for hit and runs whenever he felt he need.

"So tell me Jason, what you here for? Really?" She asked taking the blunt from his mouth in mid-pull.

She always called him by his government name when she was in a serious mood. Booman started to believe moving over here would be harder than he thought.

"I told you I just wanted to check in on my son and baby momma, is something wrong with that?" He asked, feigning shock.

Kareema laughed, "We both know the only time you come over here is to get some pussy, or run from the police. Our son has never been high on your list of priorities, so run that game on another one."

Booman checked the time on his iPhone and realized he didn't have time for a long drawn out argument about his shortcomings as a father. He already knew he wasn't a good father, but how could he possibly know how to do that when he never had a father. He had to meet up with some people about the business he needed to take care of anyway.

"Look, I know I've never been a good father to Jason, but I am here because I realized that I don't want my son to grow up and not know me."

That statement was only partially true. He wanted little man to know he was his daddy, just didn't always want the responsibility of having to provide for him and Kareema. Shit shorties were expensive, even he knew that.

Kareema twisted her lips in a smirk that said, yeah right. Seeing that she wasn't really buying it, he decided to be upfront with her.

"Look, I know I've not always provided for my son that is why I don't come around too often. Who wants to see their daddy when all he is holding out is empty hands?"

"It's not about the money Jason, it's about the time and effort you put into raising your son. He is too young to care about what you can do for him. He is more worried about you actually being present." She replied.

Booman thought he knew where this conversation was leading, it was the same conversation that always made him angry enough at Kareema to leave out the door. She didn't understand what it was like to have a daddy that when he did come around left your mother with nothing but a wet ass and another mouth to feed. Only after he had used her for a warm meal and a few dollars, did his father make a hasty exit.

Today was different though, he needed Kareema to let him move in for this plan to work and he was not ready to tell Timmo his plan didn't work. The money he stood to make hinged upon Kareema being down with him so he had to make it happen.

"Well Kareema, now I have the time and money, and I plan on being around a lot more for him, and you." He lied.

Kareema was slowly starting to feel the relaxing side effects of the weed Booman had flamed up. The words he were saying were sounding good to her ears. Jason having his dad around more often, with a few extra dollars circulating around would be nice. Booman's speech and her thoughts were interrupted by his phone ringing to the tune of 2 Chain's *I'm Riding Around*.

After a quick conversation, that involved him saying he would touch down in a few minutes, Kareema's dreams of a happy family went up in smoke. Those words signaled his exit. Seeing the look on her face made Booman realize for the first time how much his absence negatively affected Kareema and ultimately his son. He had never felt that emotion before, but quickly shook it off.

"Ree, I got a quick run to make but I promise I'll be right back. When I come back me and you have some unfinished business to handle." He said with his eyes roamed over her assets, making his dick jump.

"Yea right." Kareema mumbled sarcastically. "I've heard that shit before."

"For real ma, I'll be back in a few hours and we can finish this conversation about making us a real family."

"Well why are you taking your bag with you?" Kareema asked suspiciously.

She knew that nigga was not coming back tonight, maybe not ever. He knew that if he left right now Kareema might not buzz him up when he came back, so he decided to leave some insurance. He took every dollar of the twenty five hundred he carried on him minus fifty and told her he would be back, if for nothing else but to collect his bread. As he placed the money in her hands Kareema was shocked. That was a definite sign that he was coming back tonight, Booman was too cheap and untrusting to leave his cash with her unless he was coming back. He trusted Kareema to a certain extent and knew there was no way she could spend that all tonight, especially with all the stores being closed. Before leaving, he told Kareema to give him the key so he wouldn't wake her up when got in, it might be late. Reluctantly she took her key off the ring and handed

114

it to him. He had never asked for the key before and she had never offered. After closing the door behind him Kareema smiled, she didn't know if it was the weed or knowing that she would not have to explain to little man in the morning why his daddy left.

When Booman stepped out of the building it was like the streets had come alive. The city park a few blocks away where he was to meet up with the shorty he had recruited to push the product was alive with various groups of young men and a few females, hanging outside drinking, smoking and horse playing.

The contents of the book bag he carried made him nervous. He used to hang over here with his cousin before he got locked up back in the day, but these weren't really his stomping grounds. Booman had made a few friends, but he had stepped on more toes. The real reason he stopped coming out this way so often was because he had stepped on the wrong toes one day and was issued an ultimatum not to come back over east, or else he would lose his life. He chose life, and had to stop seeing his son.

He was fortunate that a few weeks ago the person who issued his death warrant was gunned down in the club, after disrespecting one of C-low's main men. To him it was a sign that he could come over east and not have to worry about death looming over his head. Booman reached for his phone to see where the person he was coming to meet was at. He hated being out here with this product in the book bag. It made him nervous to think of the consequences if he got robbed. He knew Timmo would murk him for all that dough.

"Hey Boo." A male voice called out from the area where the swings used to be.

All that sat was the metal structure the swings were supposed to hang from. The city never thought about replacing the swings or even tearing down the unsafe structure. It was just another reminder that no one cared about the children in America's ghettos. Booman looked up and saw who he was waiting for. He had been waiting for his cousin Amir, who was aunt's youngest son, but by no means was he to be considered a baby. He had been in the streets since he was eleven years old and his mom became addicted to crack. His two older siblings were already out of the house. His oldest sister left home at fifteen to move to Minnesota with her father's family. While his older brother was currently serving time on a twenty year armed robbery sentence he caught when he was nineteen.

Amir had started out stealing small items, like junk food, from the corner store and clothes. When his older brother found out he had a knack for stealing, he introduced him to the spoils of real theft. B and E's, snatching purses, and stealing other people's packs, eventually lead to sticking up dude's for their jewels and money, even a carjacking or two. Now Amir was considering helping Booman and himself make a few dollars.

"Hey cousin." Booman greeted him. "Long time, no see."

"Yeah I ain't seen you around here since the shit you pulled with C-Low's man. Didn't expect to see you around here anytime soon my nig." Amir chuckled.

"Them niggas didn't put no fear on my heart." Booman said with more bravado than he felt.

If dude wouldn't have ended up stinking, he wouldn't be over here. That coupled with the lure of the money to be made, helped to quell his fears of death at a young age.

"Alright man let's get out this park and handle this business. All of these people outside make me nervous."

Amir and Booman made the short trek to some chick's house that Amir was screwing. When the girl opened the door, Booman was shocked by the high end electronics that were in the front room. A 60 inch Sony Smart TV that was so large it took up an entire wall, and a surround sound system the included top of the line Bose speakers

116

hung in all four corners of the front room, as well as a few on the floor. The female who leased the apartment had yet to show her face but her presence could be felt from a bra slung over the back of the leather couch and a few other feminine items strewn across the room.

Amir led Booman to the cramped kitchen located in the back of the apartment.

"So, you got a business proposition for me? I'm gonna let you know now, I ain't into no nickel and dime bullshit. I can make more money taking from a drug dealer than selling their product." Amir said.

Before he could finish what he was saying Booman emptied the contents of his book bag on the tiny kitchen table. Amir's eyes lit up as he did a quick calculation of how much that product weighed and the estimated street value he could get for it. Hell, if Booman wasn't his auntie's son, he probably would have murked his ass for those bundles of slightly off white product. He could look at it and tell it was butter and the cash to be made was a very decent amount. After a few moments of silence Amir spoke up.

"I don't really deal in drugs cousin, that shit gets you too much time. I would much rather take from the dealers."

Booman knew this was Amir's way of laying down his terms of this business venture. Booman was ready to cut him in no more than twenty percent, but was hoping for ten.

"I know you don't sell bags on the corner fam, but you do know who I can holler at to move some weight out here. With the supply I've got, you definitely won't be standing on no one's corner. Ya feel me?"

"I'm gonna need thirty percent off top." Amir stated bluntly. "Just sitting in the kitchen with this shit will get us life my man. I don't know about you, but I like to be able to move around."

Shit, I gotta give this nigga the whole twenty, Booman thought. "Twenty percent and that my final offer. I cut you in because you are family, I can find another nigga who wants to get this paper."

Amir was smart enough to know that Booman only came to him because he had nowhere else to go. He was also smart enough to know that dope was big business, and the ones who made the money were the ones who pushed weight. Amir would know those were the kind of niggas he stuck up. Pouring them both a shot, Amir thought on it for a second.

"I can work with that."

With that he lifted his shot glass and toasted to a new family venture.

CHAPTER 11

The Streets are talking

It only took a few weeks before the money started flowing in for Booman and Amir. At first it had been a little slow. First, people were hesitant to fuck with Amir knowing his chosen profession. Second, most of the people were copping from C-Low and remained loyal because his crew had top quality product, or they feared him. However, once the shit Amir and Booman were pushing hit the block, the fiends were lined up wherever the dealers sold the dope with the black sharks on the seals. Whether it was weed, crack, or heroin, those sharks let you know it was that fire.

"If I would've known selling drugs would be this lucrative, I would have traded in my ski mask long ago." Amir commented, as him and Booman drove toward one of the trap spots to pick up some money.

"It ain't always this easy cuz." Booman said, hitting a blunt. "If you don't have a good, steady connect, you will be nickel and diming it until you cross the penitentiary doors. I just happened to know a few people."

Booman smiled to himself as he thought about his good fortune in meeting Timmo. That dude was from out west and had major connections. Booman knew once he dropped that first duffle bag of money off to him ahead of schedule, he had shown Timmo he knew how to get money and not fuck with his cash flow.

The trap house this month was at a neighborhood chick's rundown apartment on 70th and Coles. Quayla was your everyday hood rat with a house full of kids from different father's, no high school education, and looking for the next street star to father her next kid. Amir knew her from around the way, he used to hit that on really drunk nights when he need his dick sucked for free. She had tried to hint at them being something more than what it was, but he had quickly put her in her place. What they had was business, he hit her with bread sometimes when he needed a place to drop off his stolen items, or lay low when the block was hot.

Quayla thought better of cussing him out for being so blunt with her when she remembered all the extra money he helped her bring in. Hell, she had four kids under the age of twelve that needed shit. Shit that bullshit ass aide check didn't cover, plus she needed money to hang out on the weekends and put money one two of her baby daddy's books. She looked at the bright side of the situation, at least she didn't have to fuck him nigga for cash. So, she and Amir had remained business partners since that time.

When Amir walked through the door Quayla handed him the duffle bag and told him she needed some more seals. She had run out of the shark printed bags last night and hadn't bagged up the rest of the cookie she had cooked up. Booman reached into his pocket and tossed her a bag with one thousand seals.

"You should be straight with that until we roll through later." Amir said, handing her a small cut for allowing them to use her house and her cooking and bagging up skills.

After leaving the house Booman and Amir parted ways, Booman heading out south to see Timmo and Amir going to make a drop somewhere. Booman hopped on the train at 79th and begin to think about what he was going to do with all the money he had been able to make in the last few weeks. He had never seen that much money at once. In just a few short weeks he had netted twenty five stacks, and that was after he went on a spending spree with his baby momma, and made it rain dollars at the Factory. For the first time Booman was able to see all those dreams of being a big time hustler come to fruition. The only reason he had been able to hold those twenty five stacks is that he had dreams of going in the Lexus dealership and buying whatever he wanted straight cash.

That was on his agenda in the next few days, he was tired of riding the train every day and paying for cabs. It was also dangerous to be on the train with cash and product. It was safe in the aspect you were out of the way of legal harm, but every day citizens would steal your phone, purse and book bag if they thought something of value was contained inside. He most definitely had something that he could not afford to get stolen, another man's money, and Timmo had already made it clear that Booman's life would be the price for his product.

Yep, this is definitely my last day on the train, Booman thought as he got off at 95th to catch the Number 34.

****

Amir could not believe that his ratchet ass cousin had finally found a lucrative business, and he was living better than he had in his life. Although he was making a nice percentage off the take, Amir was making more money than Booman because he had been paying Quayla to cut the shit one extra time and sell it to the clucks that always came short, you know with $7.00 instead of $10.00 when they knew there was money to be made. Amir didn't like to turn any dollars away, so he decided to make a few extra dollars. Quayla had no idea what he was doing, as long as she got her small cut she didn't give a shit.

Amir turned up 2Chainz as he pulled into the parking lot of the barber shop. He was about to get lined up because tonight it was going to be juking at the Factory. The stripper Pinky was headlining tonight and the club was bound to be packed. It was still early, but he wanted to be on point when he hit the club. Shit, he still had to go find a fresh outfit from the Prada store. He was gonna be fresh to death tonight.

Yeah Booman, good looking little cuz. Good looking, he thought.

****

Something wasn't sitting quite right with C-low. He had begun to notice that his weekly profits were decreasing slowly. It hadn't taken that long for him to catch on. Since the twins had blessed him with his own piece of land over east he had a steady increase in profits, it didn't take a genius to realize someone was fucking with his money. Shit just wasn't adding up. None of his spots had been hit lately and none of his workers or soldiers had come up short, but there was still a decrease in the profits. None of that made sense to him. C-low didn't play about his paper and he planned on getting to the bottom of the situation, if it was the last thing he did.

****

Amir sat in Vert's Barbershop on 83rd and Jefferies patiently waiting to get lined up. Vert's was the spot to get a fresh cut, catch up on hood gossip and even pick up a bootleg movie or two. After hours you could always find a few regulars kicking the Bo Bo's and getting it in like they were at the club, but Amir was not one of the regulars.

Barbershops were one of Amir's favorite places to scope out potentially victims for his robbery game. When the do boys came in, they always had ice dripping from every limb and lobe stunting for the masses. These were just the type of niggas that had made him hood rich, but today Amir had just come in to get lined up. He didn't need to rob mofo's to eat. Booman had introduced him to a better way to eat. Although he wasn't a drug dealer by profession, Amir could see how the money could become addicting.

After waiting about an hour or so, the barber indicated Amir was next in line. Amir saw this as the perfect time to relieve his bladder of some of that Remy he had been drinking that morning. Making his way through the shop to the cramped bathroom in the back, Amir took notice that someone had been blowing in the bathroom, because they window was open a quarter of the way. Not wanting to piss with his back to an open window Amir walked over to close it when he noticed the voices of two men outside having a conversation. From the way the bathroom windowed was angled, the

122

men couldn't see him because the view was blocked by the backstairs of the building. Amir couldn't see their faces but he could see the shoes of the men and hear their conversation.

"So did you find out what is going on with my money?" The man with the black gators on asked.

"The word on the street is that there are some dudes from out south trying to set up shop around here."

"They say their shit is off the chain, you could cut it 3 times and still kill a hype due to a nose bleed."

"So who the fuck is this nigga?" Black Gators asked angrily.

"That's the thing, nobody knows who this nigga is. He just supplies motherfuckers that don't fuck with us and a few that do. That nigga got a brand out here."

"A brand? Who the fuck is this nigga, Jay-Z?" With that man number two handed the gator man something from his pocket. By this time Amir was on his toes trying to see what had transpired between the two men.

"What the fuck is this nigga? Everybody got seals?"

Before the dude could finish his statement the sound of police coming down the alley made them cut their meeting short. Just as Amir went to completely shut the window, he saw what the man had handed the man wearing the gators. A plastic seal with black Mako sharks floated past the window.

If Amir had to pee before he surely had to pee now. His adrenalin was pumping, he knew that the men in having the conversation were referring to Booman and him. The good thing was that they didn't know who they were. The bad thing was they would eventually find out, and he and Booman didn't have any army of niggas to back them up like C-low. All they had was each other and whomever Booman's connect was.

Amir knew that in order for this thing to lay out in him and Booman's favor they needed to be ready to go to war, and that is exactly what he planned on doing. He didn't even realize he had walked out of the shop without a lining until he was on the E-way headed out south to catch up with Booman.

While Amir decided it was time to prepare for war, Booman was deciding it was time to prepare for the life of a baller. He and Kareema had just driven a brand new, used Lexus off the lot. Well Kareema had driven it off the lot. The only reason Booman had brought her along was because his trifling ass didn't have a license, and didn't plan on getting one anytime soon. He had to put the car in someone's name and at this point she was the only one he trusted enough.

The dealer who sold them the car smiled at Kareema as she drove away.

Only a drug dealer would pay full price for a car with no haggling, he thought to himself. Better for him though, he knew if they were satisfied, they would bring more drug dealing friends in there and he could make a killing. He just hope when it was time to trade that in they came back to him.

Kareema couldn't believe that Booman had made good on a promise this important. She knew this had to be the first time that had ever happened, because she couldn't remember any other time he ever came through. Whomever he was dealing with now was pushing major weight and it showed. He had actually bought her a Lexus! Yes, it was used, and yes she understood the game he was running about it being her car, but she was still excited that he had come through. Little Jason needed him to be there.

As soon as she was getting into the groove of driving her new car, Booman asked her pull over at Mickey D's.

"Let me drive the whip Ree."

"Why, you ain't even got a license, plus didn't you say this was my car?"

He knew he was going to have to hear this shit from her, so he decided to wait until they got to her house for the argument. He had plans that night and that Lexus was definitely included in them.

"Alright girl, pick up lil man and let's go home."

When they arrived at Kareema's building, Booman helped her get Jason and his things out of the car.

"Hey Ree, let me see those keys right quick, I just want to grab some blunts and a bottle from the store."

Kareema knew he was lying, but she didn't want to argue in front of Jason so she sucked her teeth, rolled her eyes and handed him the keys.

"Bring my shit back in one piece!" She hollered as he skirted off down the street.

He needed to catch up with Amir, today was payday. Amir had been blowing up Booman's phone since he left the barbershop, to no avail. After about thirty minutes of back to back calls, Amir remembered what day it was, payday. He knew exactly where Booman was. The Factory.

Booman hadn't heard his phone ringing or vibrating since he entered the club. Although it was the middle of the afternoon, there was a decent crowd present. Tonight was going to be the night Pinky was headlining and any niggas that had seen one of her pornos definitely wanted to see her live and up close. Some must've been hoping to catch a glimpse of her before her performance tonight, but it wasn't gonna happen.

Booman was too busy blowing his cash on Roxy and Honey, two of the club's top dancers who worked the dayshift, to pay attention to the phone ringing in his pocket. Not while Roxy was shaking her ass in his face, and Honey was fondling his balls. Whoever it was could wait.

"Damn baby, you got a pipe between your legs," Honey said seductively as she grinded on Booman's rock hard dick. Roxy was busy whispering freak shit in his ear so they could relieve him of some of that cash in the VIP room.

"Both of us Daddy, but it's gonna cost you a little extra." Roxy said licking Booman's earlobe trying to con him out of some of that cash in his pockets.

Booman had decided he had spent enough money to watch now he wanted to touch, taste, and fuck. He didn't care what the price was, these freaks were gonna suck him dry for the money he had already given them. They had made a three days' worth of tips after what he just tricked off in thirty minutes. He planned on getting what he paid for.

Just as he was about to head up to VIP with the girls, Amir entered the club and gestured him over.

Shit, he thought.

"I'll be right back, I got some business to handle first." He said, smacking Roxy so hard on her ass it began to ripple.

"Okay Daddy, don't forget us." Honey said, as she walked away to the next guy wanting a lap dance.

The two strippers had made twenty five hundred off Booman in such a short time. He wanted to let them know he was balling so instead of little faces, he was tipping big faces, and when they mutually decided to double team his pockets, he didn't stand a chance. He should be happy Amir saved him from those two scheming tramps who had made plans to relive him of all his dough.

"Hey fam." Amir said greeting Booman with the Blackstone handshake. "I gotta holler at you about something."

"I got your cut right in the whip." Booman started, thinking Amir was talking about his money.

Booman was ready to get back to them bitches as he watched them across the room grinding on other niggas. That shit had him fumed after he tricked off so much.

Following his cousins eyes Amir said, "Nigga, get your head out them hoes' ass and listen to what I got to say."

Hearing the serious tone of Amir's voice, Booman instantly listened up.

"What's going on?"

"The streets is talking and we seem to be the topic of conversation." With that Amir told Booman what he had heard at the barbershop.

CHAPTER 12

Moving out South

Several things had happened in the last few weeks since Mako began to get money over east. Mako began to make money hand over fist. He and Timmo were usually profitable when it came to their ventures, but none had been as profitable as this one. He knew it was time to implement stage two of his plan. Also, as he began to spend more time with Tasha, he found himself falling hard for her.

He had never met a woman that had her own and didn't need shit from him, but his time and attention. Although he had never had an issue when it came to being able to financially take care of a woman he cared about, until Tasha there was never a woman he could say he cared about. He knew she didn't need him financially, but to know she needed him emotionally made him feel some kind of way. He was gonna take care of his boo to the fullest and provide her with the life she was accustomed to. If any man could do it, he could.

If the money they were getting over east was any indication how much they would be getting out south, he was ready to go forward and no one would stop him. After hearing what was good from Timmo via Booman, Mako realized this was not a regular get rich quick scheme him and Timmo were used to. He realized he had to be in this for the long run. With that being said, he knew it was time to stop playing in these streets and get his army up.

He allowed Timmo to handle the recruitment on his end when it came to find goon ass, thoroughbred niggas. When it came to their business arrangements he understood his strengths and weaknesses. He had more at stake than Timmo, but knew Timmo had his back at all cost, and could sniff a bitch nigga out on introduction. He trusted his judgment more than anyone, except for his Uncle Terry and grandfather.

Mako knew it was time to get ready for war. He knew once he stepped foot in the twins' territory, it would be on and popping and only the strong would survive. Mako planned on coming out on top. He knew that with Timmo behind him they could win. That nigga had the drive, loyalty, and Mako's paper behind him; there would be no stopping them. They had a meeting later that night to discuss the plan and to get ready to move. Mako was excited as could be, he was ready.

Mako turned on the TV and rolled a blunt. His grandfather would be on this afternoon to announce his candidacy for the mayoral election Mako was proud of his grandfather and excited for him. He knew Abraham had waited most of life for this opportunity, and he truly deserved it. Mako made himself a sandwich while he waited for the channel 7 news broadcast to come on.

Macon lit his blunt and made it to the TV as they were announcing his grandfather. He listened through the boring speech he'd heard countless times before and heard his granddad announce his candidacy. It was when they asked Abraham who would be his campaign manager that Mako chocked on the smoke from his blunt.

"And have you decided who will be your campaign manager in your run for mayor?" A reporter from the Sun-Times asked.

"Yes I have," Abraham said clearing his throat. He looked directly into the camera and replied, "I am proud to announce that my grandson Macon will be the manager in my campaign for mayor of this great city."

With that Abraham ended his impromptu press conference and Mako was returned back to regularly scheduled programming.

"What the fuck?" Mako yelled.

His granddad was throwing enormous salt on his enterprise by designating him to be his campaign manager. He hadn't asked for the position, and didn't want it, so he was wondering what possessed his grandfather to say he would be the one to run the campaign. When he dialed his grandfather's number, he kept getting the voicemail. He wanted to know why he hadn't been told of his grandfather's plans for his future. Shit, he had his own plans and they didn't involve running a political campaign. When he finally got through to Abraham an hour later, he couldn't even get a word out.

"We will talk when I get home." Abraham spoke calmly and then hung up the phone.

Mako was fuming that his grandfather had blown him off like that. He understood he was probably answering questions, rubbing elbows and all that shit, but Mako had never agreed to be a part of that boring ass life Abraham chose to lead. He would have to talk to his grandfather ASAP! Mako had a meeting with Timmo and some of their new generals tonight to make plans on moving into the twins' territory. He didn't have time to wait for his grandfather to come home and explain why he had done what he did. Mako knew his grandfather wasn't slow, he knew how Mako got down in the streets, so why would he put him in that position?

After Abraham had shaken the last hand, and made the last under the table business deal, he got in the car and let his driver take him home. On the way home he thought about the decision he had made to put Macon as the head of his campaign. This could either go really well or really wrong, but he trusted his grandson to do the right thing and make him a winner. This would show him what type of man he had raised Macon to be. He was hoping that it was a smart man, someone who knew how to play the game of politics as well as the game on the streets.

A few hours had passed by the time Abraham got home, and Macon had left. He'd left a note that he would be back later and he couldn't wait to talk to him. Abraham had to chuckle, he knew Macon was upset and surprised by his decision. This was a conversation he looked forward to. He settled down in his study, poured himself a drink and thought about his future.

The meeting with Timmo and their soldiers went well. Everyone was in lace and had the tools they needed to complete the task tomorrow night. After everyone had left, Mako told Timmo the story of what Abraham had decided for his future today.

"I heard." Timmo chuckled. "Guess Pops doesn't know you have plans of your own."

"Yeah, I hate to disappoint him, but I got other plans." Mako said, taking the blunt for his friend.

"What you mean?" Timmo asked puzzled. "This is all the better for our plans."

"As long as your granddad runs the city, we will be untouchable! With him as the mayor and his grandson as the biggest street hustler this mug has ever seen, shit couldn't be sweeter."

Mako had never thought about it from this angle. With his grandfather running the city he would have every politician, police officer, and alderman in the city at his disposal. As long as he presented himself in the light as an upstanding citizen, he would be able to move silently in the streets.

"Man your ass be on shit I don't even think of T. You definitely the trigger to my gun nigga." Mako said giving his boy dap.

Timmo just shook his head as he hit the blunt. *This nigga definitely was bred in the streets*, he thought. *He should have seen the positive in that situation years ago. Guess it takes a street nigga like me to make him see the light.*

"Welcome to my world nigga." Timmo said passing the blunt.

"In a few days, the beginning of our rule in these streets will start." Mako boasted.

Timmo realized that once they set up shop out south, there would be no turning back. This would be the ultimate test for them both, the test of a true boss. This would be life and death for them and Timmo hoped they were both up to task. He may have been a goon and a killer, but he knew his best friend was none of those things. He was the muscle and he was cool with that, somebody had to crack heads, but he didn't think Mako understood the importance of this venture to him. This was the opportunity of his lifetime.

****

"Get up Kris." He said, smacking Kristen on the ass to awake her.

He'd just laid it down on her about an hour ago and she always had some new tricks for him. He had to smile at her. If it wasn't for her role in the takeover, the shit would be virtually impossible.

TWO WEEKS EARLIER

"I don't know about this Tim," Kristen said, "the twins don't play about their money."

Up until this point, Timmo assumed he had Kristen wrapped around his finger, he had asked her to do little things for him to see how much he could trust her, and she showed he could a little. He had never let her know his real plan up until now, she still didn't know that was his true purpose for fucking with her was. The more Timmo laid out his plan, the more terrified Kristen became. She was just trying to get a little bread, she wasn't trying to betray the twins. As he lay out his plan, a million red flags were thrown up in her brain and warning signs flashed.

"I'm not asking you to do any more than you have been. I'm just asking you to move locations."

"I'm not sure about that Timmo, my sister would kill me if she found out."

Hell, she knew the twins would kill her if they found out. They had feed her family for years and were there when she and Samantha had nothing. This would be the ultimate betrayal.

"How she gonna know if you don't tell her? That's why you are so important to this whole plan Kris. Who would suspect you of any wrong doing? This is your hood and your fam works for them niggas, you would never look suspect."

To be honest Timmo couldn't think of any more angles to get her to see things his way.

"Are you gonna say something Kris or look crazy?"

"I am trying to tell you boo, it's not a good idea. I have heard stories about the twins and how they get down when niggas decide to play with their money." Kristen warned. She wanted no parts of that drama. "With all the money we're making over east, we don't have to be greedy." Kristen said trying to encourage him to think of other ways to get paper.

Timmo had to laugh. "So whose money do you thinking we are taking over east?"

"C-low."

"Who do you think put C-low on? It is his empire, but that nigga definitely pays tithes to the twins. So you been fucking with their money all along."

Kristen's heart sank into her stomach. She was never too into hood politics, so she had no idea she had been going against the grain all along by making drops over east for Timmo.

Seeing reality hit her hard, Timmo went in for the kill. "You have already put your feet in the pool, so don't be scared to take the swim now."

Realizing there was no turning back, Kristen went home to tell Samantha she was moving out.

* * * * * * * * * * * * *

When Mako got to his grandfather's house, it was well after midnight. He assumed Pops would be sleep, but when he walked past his office, he found him awake, drinking and staring out the window.

"I wondered when you would make it in." Abraham said, setting his glass down on his oversized mahogany antique desk.

Mako didn't have time to wonder how his granddad knew he was passing by the room. Then he noticed that the cameras were on when he entered the office.

"So Macon," Abraham began, "how do you feel about your new position?"

Abraham was expecting to fight his grandson on this announcement and he was ready. He was ready to tell Macon he had no excuse to try to make a living in the streets when he had every opportunity provided to him. So when Macon didn't put up a fight he was shocked.

"It's cool Pops. I see where you are going with this. You want me to live up to the family name and get my power from legal avenues. I'm all for it."

Abraham stared at his grandson, trying to bore through his soul to see what it was he was truly thinking. Macon had never given in so easy and Abraham knew that he was not trying to be involved in his

134

political schemes. Abraham felt that it was time for Macon to grow up.

"Well that was easier than I thought. No objections to my decision then?"

"Not at all Pops. I'll be there bright and early Monday morning." Mako replied.

 With nothing more to say, the two men said good night and Mako went to his room. While Abraham's thought were on how easily his grandson gave in, his grandson's thoughts were how easy his plan was coming together.

On September 30th, Mako's plan was put into action. Seven of the twins' top earning spots were not only robbed by masked men for money, but shortly after being robbed, the locations were raided by the police for the kilos of coke that had been left in each of the spots. Not only did the twins have to deal with the loss of hundreds of thousands of dollars, they had to dish out money to bail their people out of the Cook County jail as well. Not to add that tomorrow was the first of the month and they had little dope to supply the fiends.

The first part of Mako's plan went flawlessly. By the time all the money he and Timmo had gotten from robbing the spots the twins' owned throughout Roseland added up, it more than paid for the new shipments of dope they were about to flood the streets with. The twins would never know what hit them.

CHAPTER 13

Time for War

By the time the 6:00 am news broadcast came on, Raymond and Charles had already been informed what had taken place through the night. Charles was the first one to receive a call that one of the major spots had been hit. Before he could get off the phone, he was flooded with text and calls from other generals who were informing him of their spots being hit too. This shit was too much, way too early in the morning, but Charles knew he would have to inform Raymond of what was happening. This was definitely not going to be a social call.

Raymond was livid when his brother made that phone call to tell him what was going on.

"What the fuck is going on Charles? Who the fuck has access to our spots? It's no coincidence that our most profitable spots in Roseland were hit on the same day for nothing but cash. These niggas didn't take no dope just cash. That shit just don't sit right with me!" Raymond said, slamming his fist on the desk so hard Charles swore he heard it crack. "Where the fuck was the niggas who was supposed to be on security? Tomorrow is the first and not only have we been stuck up for over six hundred thousand dollars, you mean to tell me the police run in a few hours later and raid the houses for the dope! I don't believe in coincidences. Someone set us up for the okey doke and I want to know who and how yesterday!"

Charles let his brother rant and rave. He had no choice, he felt partially to blame for the spots getting hit. Part of his job was to enforce security and make sure them little niggas was on the job. He got caught slipping. He was pissed. He had no idea who would have the balls, cash, army, or political connections to pull this off. Charles was determined to get to the bottom of this. What happened in the wee hours of the morning would hit their pockets for months to come and that shit wasn't gonna fly. Whomever these niggas were, they were going to die a slow death.

"Charles, call everyone in the inner circle together. Tell them they have two hours to get their asses to the meeting place."

"Already done brother, they should be there in an hour."

"And Charles, call C-low and tell him his presence is requested at this get together, and do not take no for an answer."

The meeting was in the basement of the Factory. No one knew there was a basement except for a select few. Raymond and Charles owned the building and had it built to their specifications. This basement was in the plans and used for meetings such as the one they were having at this moment.

The room was dimly lit and was cloudy from blunt, cigar and cigarette smoke. This room also held the most important members of the twins' crew. Al-G, who was the twins third arm, Samantha who ran the dry cleaners that laundered the most money for the enterprise, K-dub, Wet, and Killa who were generals whose spots were hit the previous night.

"Somebody in this mofo better know something!" Raymond roared, looking around the room into each of the faces of his most trusted inner circle.

He was trying to gauge if he could see any deceit in their eyes. So far, all he saw was fear, fear of not being able to answer the boss' questions. Fear of not knowing who ran up in the spots they were responsible for watching. Mostly they feared for their lives. Charles and Raymond could kill each and every one of them in that room and no one would ever know.

"C-low," Raymond spat, "can you shed some light on this situation?"

"Ray I can't give you the answers you need necessarily, but I can tell you what I noticed going on in my hood. I think we might be looking for the same niggas."

"Cut the shit and get to it nigga." Charles barked impatiently.

His trigger finger was on straight itch mode today, he was ready to leave some bodies stinking.

"Peep this," C-low began, "I started noticing a few weeks ago that profits were slowly declining. You know I stay on top of my dough. So at first I thought niggas was putting their hands in the cookie jar, but no one ever came with short money. Then I realized, it was the laws of supply and demand at work. I had the supply but the demand was not there. Someone has been selling their dope in my land and not paying their dues. I got a funny feeling these are the same niggas that hit your stash houses and set you up for the police raid."

"So who is this nigga?" Raymond asked irritated.

"That I haven't figured out yet, but I got my ears and eyes to the streets, give me a week or two and I'll have that nigga."

After it was decided on that C-low would find the niggas responsible, he excused himself from the meeting and they moved on to the next issue. Tomorrow was the first, the biggest money making day of the month and they had very little dope to move. They wouldn't be able to get a new shipment until the fifth, but after that the money making window would pass.

"Samantha, how much you got left?" Al-G asked.

"All I got is six shirts." She replied speaking in code as if she were working at the cleaners.

"That ain't gonna do shit!" Al-G said discouraged. "That's not enough to supply the spots that got hit for two hours."

"Alright, here is what we do, all those packages go to one central location. Open up shop at the apartment on 113th Place above the Chinese store." Raymond instructed.

"I want lookouts on every corner and in every store on the strip." Charles finished. "The block is extra hot today due to the raids and it being election season. Be careful, be smart and get money."

Raymond dismissed everyone and stayed back to talk to Charles.

"Brother I know you feel responsible, but this is not your fault. Whoever these little niggas is must have a death wish and I plan on granting that wish for them. I know that you are ready to crack some heads, but we have to make sure the head we crack is big enough to make an example of anyone who tries to lay us down." Raymond bellowed. "I got a feeling that whoever is behind this is not a low level soldier. Naw, whoever this is has money and an army behind them."

"I can only think of a few people who could come up against us, and one of them was in this room tonight." Charles responded.

Raymond chuckled. "My brother you are a man who has stolen the words from my very mind. Keep an eye on C-low for me. He is the only nigga with the gumption, balls, and money to go to war with me."

Charles looked confused. C-low had been sent on his own with their blessing and protection, he had made a name for himself over east, but he owed all that to the twins. Why would he betray them?

"I know what you are thinking brother," Raymond said, "but why do you think I gave C-low his own, so he would never try to come after what is ours. I just hope the plan didn't backfire on me."

With that the brothers hugged and parted ways.

****

Mako's plan had worked brilliantly. After the only spot the twins had opened on 113th Place was shut down due to lack of dope. He flooded the streets with his dope. Although the fiends knew the regular dealers were out, when it came to getting a fix it didn't matter whose crew it came from.

After hitting a cluck off with a few rocks for free, Booman made sure that he went and told the fiends around the hood that they had that fire over the tracks on 119th. Booman enlisted the help of Little Cortez and some of his buddies to move packs for them. Booman had promised Little Cortez twenty five hundred dollars if he could move the two keys Booman had started him out with. Within two hours Cortez was calling him telling him he needed more.

When Booman got two blocks away from the tip, he saw where the line started to form. There was a line of clucks around the block so long you would have thought the church was handing out free food. Booman could think that he had hit the jackpot, and then he thought all those clucks were making the spot hot. He called Cortez out to the car and gave him some more to tip. For the next four days the heart of Roseland looked like Jesus had come and raptured all of the fiends, because there was not one in sight on that side of the tracks.

Four days later, Booman, Amir, and Timmo had sold twelve keys of coke that had been stepped on, cooked and rocked up. Neither one of them had ever seen that much money at one time in their lives.

CHAPTER 14

Where Loyalties Lie

It had been a few weeks since the robbery and raid on the twins' spots. They were still trying to bounce back from all the money that was lost at the beginning of the month and figure out who was behind the caper. In the meanwhile the twins' income was dwindling at a rapid pace and no one had any answers.

Samantha counted the money again for a third time. Although every dime was accounted for, in all the years she had worked for the twins she had never seen their profits go down. Samantha was twenty seven years old now and she had been working for the twins since she was sixteen. She knew that when Al-G came to pick up the money, he was not going to be pleased.

She knew that the workers weren't the problem, they had always come correct with that cash. The few that didn't were swiftly and brutally dealt with as an example to the next person who thought they were gonna get over. Any fool with a grain of sense in the land knew better than that. Since Samantha kept the accounts for the twins, she knew where the problem lay; supply and demand.

No matter what the drug, the demand on the streets was always high. Pills, rocks, weed, heroin, you name it, but ever since the robbery and raid on the same day, it seemed like the hypes weren't buying their product anymore. What did they expect? Dope fiends' loyalty to a drug dealer lay in the quality of the product and who had it when it was needed. Unfortunately, they had the quality just not enough product. Sam had been racking her brain for weeks trying to figure out who was behind this madness.

This time last month she would have been calling Al-G for a re-up to supply the workers and now she was sitting on five bricks that hadn't moved since she got them almost two weeks ago. Her thoughts were interrupted by the phone ringing, it was Al-G.

"Good morning Roseland Washtub, how can I help?" Samantha asked in a professional tone.

Yes most of the money the cleaners made was illegal, but they did have a regular clientele who actually washed clothes and got them cleaned.

"Hello, this is Mr. Green. I was calling to see if my suits were ready for pick up." Al-G asked.

"I am sorry Mr. Green," Samantha said, "but we only have three of your suits ready, the rest are still under repair."

Al-G as quiet for a moment. "I am disappointed to hear that, but I will still come in and pick up the ones that are ready." With that he hung up the phone.

"Shit!" Samantha blurted, hanging the phone up.

She was sitting on all this work, and had no answers as to who was undercutting their business. She had been racking her brain for answers for weeks and was coming up short. She couldn't think of one person who had the clout or balls to attempt what was being done to the twins.

Samantha's train of thought was broken by the electronic beep in the back office signaling that someone had walked in the front door. Looking at the security cameras, Samantha saw that it was Al-G. She put the rest of the money away in the safe, and prepared for the conversation that was coming.

"What's good Mantha?" Al-G asked greeting her with a hug.

"Nothing's good right now, but there sure is a whole lot of bad up."

"I can tell by the numbers." Al-G said disgustedly. "So give me the rundown."

Samantha began to lay out for Al-G that customers who copped weight, half-birds and up were either not copping as much as usual, or simply had stopped buying product from them.

"This is bullshit, and we still have no idea who the fuck is behind this shit?"

"I can only speak for myself, I don't have a clue" Samantha said feeling as this was her fault in some way.

"The clock is ticking Samantha. We can't afford to take another hit next month..." Al-G was so angry he couldn't finish his sentence.

Al-G was very protective of the twins. They had been running together for over twenty years and he was often referred to as the third twin by some. He could usually be found at the side of both, when the twins were together, and when they weren't together he was riding with Raymond as his enforcer. He didn't take it lightly when someone was stealing food from his table, which happened to be Raymond and Charles' table too.

"It has got to be someone is in the inner circle, or is close to someone in the inner circle. That means we have a traitor in our mist. Do you have any idea who it could be?" Al-G asked Samantha searching her eyes for any indication she had something to do with this.

Samantha started to say, "I have no idea..." but stopped short of finishing her sentence. Something was niggling in the back of her mind.

"What you thinking Mantha?"

"That you are right. No one out south is crazy enough to go to war with us, and whoever is supplying our clientele is not from the Land. The repercussions would be too swift and brutal."

At that moment, an image of Kristen's face flashed across Samantha's mind. She instantly felt sick to her stomach.

"You okay Mantha? You look like you are about to hurl." Al-G asked suspiciously eyeing her.

"I don't know, I ate breakfast at the Ranch this morning and you know they fell off. I just need a 7-Up and I'll be good."

"Alright ma, I'll get up with you later." Al-G said walking out the office.

When he got into his whip, he thought about the conversation he had just had with Samantha, and how she seemed to be saying the right things but her actions were suspect. Al-G just hoped she didn't have anything to do with this. He loved Samantha like a sister, but he wouldn't hesitate to put a bullet in her brain for an act of disloyalty.

Whatever the issue, Al-G had a really bad feeling about how this was going to play out. Whomever had made this power play had the resources and clout to stay virtually invisible, and the more he thought on it, the less names he had on his list, and C-low was at the top of that list. He crossed him off only because his business had taken a hit as well, but still it, had been weeks and C-low hadn't produced a name like he said he would and the twins' patience was running out.

The only other person that came to mind was Abraham Clark. In his time Abraham had been like the black godfather on Chicago's west side and had been best friends with the twins' father back in the day. Now, he was into politics but that didn't mean shit in the Chi.

144

Illegal money and politics went hand and hand. Although the public image of Abraham was an upstanding citizen, Al-G would be willing to bet a million bucks that his hands were as dirty as the Calumet River. The more Al-G thought about it, he had to cross Abraham off the list, because he was the twins' godfather. Not very many people knew that. The ties that bonded the twins and Abraham ran deep, and since Abraham was the one that had put them on, it also didn't make much sense. Now he was back to square one with no suspects. He decided to keep an eye on Samantha just to make sure she wasn't the traitor.

As soon as Samantha saw Al-G pull out from the parking lot on the security cameras she called her little sister Kristen. Throughout her conversation with Al-G all she could think about was Kristen. How she moved out so abruptly, never telling Samantha where she was moving to or who she was moving with. Samantha assumed it was with some dude because Kristen didn't have a job to pay anyone's rent. All the expensive clothes Kristen had recently been getting, the jewelry, the money. It all made sense, it all fit together. Samantha just hoped that her little sister didn't have anything to do with this after all the twins had done for them.

"Come on Kris answer the phone." Samantha said as she was sent to voicemail for the fifth time.

Samantha had been born to a mother who was decent enough, but partied a lot. She unfortunately became one of the victims of the crack epidemic invading black neighborhoods. Being that her mother Carolyn had come up in the 70's where a line of coke didn't turn you into a walking zombie, she was in no way prepared for the devastation that her first puff of the crack pipe would bring.

Samantha remembered the first time she saw a crack pipe. She was in her mother's room looking being nosy as most kids are. Not looking for anything in particular, just rambling. She found a shoe box under the bed that rattled when she moved it. Being the ever curious child she opened the box and found that it contained a crack pipe, glass vials, and steel wool. Although Samantha had never seen a pipe in her life, she knew what it was, and at the age of seven her life would drastically change.

After Kristen was born a year later, the call of the crack pipe became too loud for Carolyn, who had given the drug up long enough to carry her baby, to ignore. She might have been a crack head, but she wasn't that far gone to want her children addicted to the bullshit too. After listening to Kristen scream and cry at the top of her lungs with no relief, Carolyn slipped down the slope that would lead to her life as a crack head.

By the time Samantha was sixteen, she was left alone to fend for herself and nine year old sister Kristen. She began selling drugs and Carolyn didn't care as long as Samantha kept her high, and it was a major bonus because she brought Samantha a lot of customers. One night Samantha decided she could no longer support her mother's habit. She loved her mother and every time she gave her a bag she was killing her little sister's dreams of ever having a real loving mother.

Sitting in her room with an old plate and rusty razor blade, Samantha sat up bagging up some work she had just gotten on credit. He mother had found her last pack and smoke it all up now Samantha had no money to re-up with and had to beg a mofo to be fronted. She was tired of this nickel and dime bullshit and her mother's crack head antics. She was so entranced in her thoughts and what she was doing she didn't hear Carolyn stumble in the house.

"Oooh, let me get some of those crumbs Mantha." Her mother said bursting in her room.

"No!" Samantha replied, not even looking up from what she was doing.

"How you gonna say no to me? You in my house bagging that shit up for free."

Samantha looked up from her plate and looked in her mother's face. Although Carolyn was a drug addict she still had traces of beauty from years past. Samantha could almost see the mother she once had until she took all of her in.

"I will not support your habit anymore, and that last packed you smoked up set us back. I don't know how we're gonna pay rent."

Samantha was upset that her mother was more concerned with supporting her habit than her children. Carolyn was upset Samantha was teasing her with a plate of crack in her house and had the nerve to be stingy. She was feigning and that shit her daughter had looked like a plate of gold.

"You ungrateful little bitch!" Her mother spat. "You can get the fuck out of my house or give me a hit, the choice is yours!"

"I ain't giving you shit now get out of my room Ma, I'm tired of this bullshit!"

Samantha had never disrespected her mother before, but she couldn't take another minute of the neglect and abuse she had to endure since her mother got addicted to crack. Before Samantha knew what was happening, Carolyn smacked the shit out of her. Like lightening Samantha was on her and she and her mother were fighting like two bitches in the street.

In the end Samantha woke up in the hospital. In the heat of the moment, Carolyn forgot that the person she was fighting was her daughter; she ended up stabbing Samantha three times. One of those wounds ended up inches away from her heart. Carolyn ran off with the drugs and little money Samantha had stashed in the house. The day Samantha was released from the hospital, she was found dead in the alley behind Gateley's Garage, a victim of the Roseland Rapist.

While Samantha was in the hospital, Kristen was being cared for by the next door neighbors the Johnsons. Tasha was her friend and *when her uncles heard about the madness going on across the street through their niece's tears, they decided to do something about it. The day Samantha made it home from the hospital, the twins and Tasha had welcomed her and her little sister with open arms. They had been her family ever since.*

The bond and love she felt for those two men ran deep and she thought her little sister had felt the same way. She needed her sister to have as much loyalty to the twins as she did, both of their lives depended on Kristen's loyalty.

CHAPTER 15

The Meeting

"Who knew this shit would've been so easy to pull off?" Mako said handing Timmo the blunt.

They were downtown at the W Hotel in the bar congratulating themselves on shutting Roseland down. They were also meeting to move on to phase two of their plan. The two friends were actually waiting for Booman and Amir. This would be the first time that Mako would be meeting them face to face. He wanted to stay in the shadows, but with the recent events, he felt that it was time for the leader to show his face to the generals. It was time for war, he just hoped they were ready.

"Man where these niggas at?" Mako griped, checking the time on his phone. "Money waits for no man and I got some other shit to do tonight."

"Man the only shit you got to do tonight is Tasha." Timmo chuckled while sipping his Remy.

All Mako could do was laugh, because his friend was right on point with his observation. He was really feeling Tasha. He found himself wanting to spend all his free time with her. Lavishing her with gifts and expensive dinners, jewelry or anything her heart desired made him feel warm and fuzzy inside. Though he would never admit it out loud.

"There them niggas go right there." Timmo said.

Booman and Amir walked in the hotel's bar and looked so out of place Mako couldn't help but to shake his head. As soon as they sat down Timmo started.

"Let's get to the introductions."

Once everyone was introduced the four men got down to business.

"Amir in order for this to work you and Booman have got to have all your soldiers in place." Mako advised.

"The twins are going to be waiting for some bullshit to jump off in the G.

"Man those niggas in Altged Gardens hold the twins down to the fullest." Booman interjected. "They got block two and four locked on the crack game. Blocks seventeen, eleven and one are the weed spots, and blocks three, five, and seven is where the dope spots are at."

"Man how the fuck you know all the business?" Timmo interrupted.

He still didn't trust Booman. Once again this nigga knew too much about everybody's fucking business. Booman laughed.

"The twins aren't the only niggas with eyes and ears to the streets."

In actuality, Amir had a bitch he fucked with that lived in block two. Her brothers and cousins both were soldiers for the twins' enterprise and once Amir laid that nine inch pipe on her and laced her up with some bread, she started talking. She was his inside to the Gardens, but he wasn't telling these niggas that.

During the whole conversation Amir had been very observant. Only speaking if he was spoken too and answering questions with one word answers when possible. He was watching these two cats very closely. He knew Booman and himself were making a killing, so these two cats had to be rolling in crème. He could tell Mako had that Guap just by looking at the way he dressed and carried himself, and it was something about this nigga that was familiar, but he just couldn't put his finger on it.

"Amir? Why you so quiet my man you are the one handling the man power so how is that looking?" Mako asked him.

Mako had been wondering why this nigga was so quiet. He didn't trust a nigga that didn't say too much, because that meant he was watching everything closely.

"We good Jo. I got twelve little hungry soldiers ready to make rank and that paper. You just make sure we got the firepower we need to make this shit happen."

Mako stared Amir down. He didn't like this nigga. He didn't trust this nigga. He didn't trust Booman either, but Booman didn't have the heart to purposefully become a thorn in Mako's side. This nigga right here did. The look in Amir's eyes was cold and calculating and during the conversation it looked like he was trying to figure something out, like he was plotting. Yeah, he was definitely going to tell Timmo to watch that nigga closely.

Meanwhile on the other side of town Raymond and Charles were having a meeting of their own. In the basement of the Factory the core group of people responsible for the twins' enterprise sat at the table. It was like déjà vu from a few weeks prior, same place, same time, same people, with the exception of C-low.

"This shit has gotten out of hand!" Raymond roared.

"Just about every major dealer we supplied in Roseland has slowly stopped buying our product."

"We need to lay down the law in these streets and let them know if it ain't come from us, a nigga ain't selling shit!" Al-G angrily stated.

"Man it's too close to the election to let the gutter run red with blood." Charles said. "We need to be smart about this shit. If we start killing motherfuckers its only gonna bring heat to our family and none of us need that kind of attention."

Everyone at the table nodded their heads in unconscious agreement. Nobody wanted a war. War meant money stopped flowing, and good soldiers would be lost. That was bad for business on all fronts, but if it was inevitable, the twins were ready.

"Well what the fuck are we supposed to do?" Al-G questioned, standing up from the table. "Let these punk motherfuckers ride with that shit?"

"Calm down bro," Raymond said, placing a firm hand on Al-G's shoulder. "I got the situation..."

Raymond's sentence was interrupted by a buzzer letting them know someone was on their way downstairs. Charles looked at the security camera, saw it was C-low and let him in. When Charles opened the door, C-low could feel the tension and anger flowing out of the room.

"What's good?" C-low greeted Charles

"What's good better be whatever you have to say."

Once the door closed behind C-low all eyes were on him. He knew and loved every nigga in the room, but the look in their eyes said they would tear his ass to pieces if he didn't have an answer to their question. Who was it?

"What's the business C?" Raymond asked, cutting to the chase.

"A few days ago two of my workers ran into a shorty that used to serve for me. He was always short when it came time to collect, so I shot his ass down on the supply side."

"Get to what I want to hear!" Raymond snarled impatiently, not in the mood to indulge C-low in his story time.

"I'm getting there big bro give me a sec. Anyway, so one of my guys see him posted up on the block, when they go to shorty to see what's up, he breaks out running. To make a long story short they whip shorty's ass until he says who's supplying him. He ends up giving them these." C-low said, throwing the shorty's pack on table.

The zip lock bag was full of nickel bag seals with black sharks printed on the front of them.

"So what the fuck are we supposed to do with that?" Al-G asked. "Everybody bags up in seals nigga."

"You are right G, but not everyone uses these seals. I've seen these before out in K-town. I got a cousin out there who is on the grind and he fucks with a cat who calls himself Mako, like the shark."

There was a collective sigh of relief from the majority of the room's occupants. Samantha's sigh was one of relief, she now knew Kristen had nothing to do with it. The dude she fucked with was named Timmy, Timmo or some shit like that, nothing resembling a shark. Al-G sighed because now he knew who was about to pay the piper, and he didn't have to suspect Samantha anymore. The other people sighed because the suspicion was off them and on the real culprit.

However, neither Raymond nor Charles breathed a sigh of relief. If anything, what C-low had just told them only made the situation worse. The brother exchanged knowing looks that were ignored by everyone in the room, but Al-G. He knew what those seals meant and knew nothing good would come of the situation. Everyone began to file out the room once they knew what their specific task was.

Charles pulled C-low to the side.

"Hey, here is something to hit your worker's hand with, that information was priceless my man."

With a nod of his head C-low went to make his exit.

"Hey where is shorty you caught serving that shit?" Charles inquired ready to tie up loose ends if need be.

"Oh he decided to take a swim in the Calumet." C-low said, laughing as he walked out the door.

"You ready to make that ride brother?" Raymond asked Charles. "It's time we paid our godfather a visit."

****

Abraham sat in the den of his beautifully restored Oak Park home. He had built a fire in the fire place, not because it was cold, but because it reminded him of home. As he sipped his Remy he was drawn to the pictures of his family around the room. There were many different eras of pictures in here, but you could tell the rise to power he made just by looking at the progression of the pictures.

As Abraham picked up the old photograph of his parents, his smile was bittersweet. His parents had been poor sharecroppers on a Mississippi plantation which had owned previous generations of his father's family. In the photograph his father was wearing a pair of overalls, Abraham laughed at that. It was the only thing he ever saw his father wear. A poor farmer had no need for fancy clothes or even pictures, but he remembered his mother had scrimped and saved just for a one time memory of her family etched on paper.

She wore her best dress in this photo, she only had three, two to work in and one for Sundays. The funny thing is, neither of his parents wore smiles in the picture. I guess back then there wasn't too much for a poor black man to smile about in Mississippi.

At his age, he understood he was born in a time in which it was a badge of honor to kill a black man in Mississippi. He quickly learned a foot would always be on his neck, and a black man would never be allowed to prosper, as he watched the cotton mill cheat his illiterate father out of his hard earned harvest.

By the age of seven he had already set his sights on going north like a runaway slave, and he had finally gotten a chance to get away when his parents sent him on the train up north out of fear for his young black life. His mother cried and his father had shook his hand and given him half of his life savings which amounted to three dollars. Now he was about to be the mayor of the city of Chicago, if things went as planned. As long as Macon could stay out of the spotlight, Abraham had nothing to worry about.

As he took another sip of his drink, his thoughts were interrupted by a knock on the door.

"Mr. Clark," his maid Ms. Singleton said, "two men are at the door for you, Raymond and Charles Johnson. I told them you weren't seeing anyone but they insisted it was urgent."

Caught off guard by the twins showing up unexpected, he quickly told her to send them up. Raymond and Charles coming to see him could not be good. All he could think of was the election being a few weeks away and he didn't need any street drama to come in between him and his destiny.

Abraham could not believe how different his godsons looked. Yes, it had been many years since he had a face to face with them. It was around the time of Jackie's death and that had been a sore, tragic wound for both families.

"How are my godsons doing?" Abraham greeted them with a hug. Sensing the resistance in Charles, he asked, "So what brings you to my side of town?"

Raymond took a seat and began to tell his godfather about what was happening in the streets. The more he talked the more Abraham had the feeling his grandson had everything to do with what was going on. How many times had he told that hardheaded boy to let sleeping dogs lie? When Raymond was finished, Abraham cleared his throat before he spoke.

"I want both of you to know that in no way did I sanction this. I gave up the game years ago to pursue my political career. On the other hand I have a grandson who can't seem to resist the call of the streets."

"Streets that don't belong to him." Charles cut in.

"Charles." Raymond said, trying to appease his brother's anger.

"As I was saying," Abraham continued, "consider this issue squashed. I will deal with Macon on my end and I appreciate you allowing me the chance to handle the situation instead of handling it yourselves."

On the outside, Abraham displayed a calm, collected demeanor, yet inside his blood was boiling. He had had enough of Macon's games. Now he was playing with the livelihood of the Clark legacy and Abraham would not tolerate it.

As the twins got up to leave Abraham spoke.

"Your father was my best friend, my brother, and when you two were born I promised him I would always look out for you and your mother if something ever happened to him. All a black man has in this world is his word and his balls and I was never known for breaking either."

Raymond acknowledged him with a nod of his head and walked out the door. Abraham heard the grandfather clock chime, signaling that it was time to get ready for a dinner that was being held for him by some political constituents. Macon had to be present at the dinner, so Abraham decided he would talk to him afterwards about retreating from Roseland.

CHAPTER 16

It All Makes Sense

"Mako, I don't even know what to wear to a political constiu...whatever party you trying to take me too." Tasha whined.

"I told you I was taking you to dinner tonight right?"

"Yeah, but I didn't know that was what you meant."

"Tasha, it doesn't matter what you wear baby you're gonna be the finest thing in that joint."

Tasha wanted to go but she didn't want to have dinner and feel like she as being judged or watched. Mako assured her it wasn't like that. The people attending were people who donated generously to his grandfather's campaign, and since he was the campaign manager, he had to show his face.

"Well I guess if you don't want to go I will have to find another date." Mako teased.

"Don't get fucked up!" Tasha warned, smacking him in the back of the head with a pillow.

"Come on T, I'll take you shopping for a new dress if you go."

"I can buy my own dress."

"Yeah, but we all know you would rather spend my cash." Mako said laughing.

"You got that right." Tasha said getting off the couch. "You must be taking me to the Chanel store?" Mako laughed and shook his head, thankful he brought his black card with him.

When Mako and Tasha arrived at the banquet room downtown at the Palmer House Hotel, she was in awe of all the powerful people she saw in the room. There was the current mayor, who was retiring, the chief of police, influential businessmen, and some people she knew for a fact had their hands in the streets, one way or another.

The dinner was very formal. There were place cards at the tables that let everyone know where they were sitting. Mako had helped with the seating plan deciding where everyone sat depending on what business deals would help his grandfather profit. Just because Mako preferred the street game to the political game, didn't mean he wasn't able to play the political game. Shit, he had learned from one of the very best.

Of course he and Tasha were seated at the main table with his grandfather and a few important VIP's on the campaign staff. During dinner conversation was polite and a lot of the topics went over Tasha's head because she didn't give a fuck about politics. Hell, she didn't even vote, wasn't even registered, but after seeing how the political machine worked up close and personal, she decided she was going out to register Monday morning.

"So tell me what line of work are you in Tasha?" Abraham's female acquaintance asked her.

"Oh, I do a little of this and that, but fashion is where my heart is. I am planning on opening up a boutique that sells the best and latest fashions from Europe." Tasha explained.

Mako gave her a wink that said good thinking baby girl. Tasha was a good observer, she knew these people would start asking questions and she didn't want to embarrass Mako or herself. Eventually the conversation Tasha was having delved into more personal issues.

"So what do your parents do?" Eva, who was Abraham's date, asked.

"Well unfortunately I never knew my father, and my mother passed away when I was very young."

Good thinking, Mako thought to himself as he began eating his sirloin. *Throw them off tell them parents are dead so they stop asking questions. My baby is made for this shit.*

"Oh, I am sorry to hear that." Eva said.

"Oh, it's okay I was lucky enough to be raised by my uncles. They have always made me feel loved and provided for me well."

Abraham's ears perked up, "Tasha, where did you grow up?"

"On the south side of Chicago."

"Oh, I know a few people out that way where about?"

What the fuck, Mako thought. *Granddad hasn't said more than three words to her since we got here, now he is so interested in her life story. What is he up to,* Mako wondered.

"I thought this was a dinner not a game of twenty questions." Mako joked. Trying to throw the heat off Tasha, as he shot Abraham a quizzical look.

"Excuse me for being so intrusive, I just figured maybe she knew someone familiar." Said Abraham casually playing his curiosity off.

Mako didn't buy it for a second. The rest of dinner went smoothly and Tasha was excited that Mako had let her glimpse into the life that he lived. She had always thought he got his money from selling drugs, but now she realized his paper was legit and politically connected.

On their way out Tasha was stopped by Eva and Abraham. "Tasha, can I have your last name so when you open up that boutique

I can look you up? If you have any items that compare to what you were wearing tonight I would love to be your first customer."

"Johnson, Natasha Johnson, and let me give you my phone number too."

Upon hearing the last name Johnson, Abraham immediately stiffened. Macon noticed his grandfather's slight change in demeanor and wondered what that was all about. While the women exchanged numbers, Abraham pulled Macon to the side and let him know he needed to speak with him tonight about something very important.

"Can it wait until the morning Pops? I'm tired and I've got to drop Tasha off back out south?"

"No it can't. I expect you at my house in two hours. No questions."

Mako started to protest, but it was something about the way Abraham's voice sounded, he knew he was dead serious.

"Alright Eva, are you ready?"

"Yes, and it was nice meeting you again Tasha."

"Baby, I am so happy I let you drag me to this dinner." Tasha giddily told Mako.

"Why? It's the same old boring ass people I have to see now that my granddad got me as this campaign manager."

"Baby, you opened my eyes to a completely different level of the game." Tasha said, kissing him on the lips.

"No baby you opened me up to another side of the game with your classic story on your parents being dead. Good way to throw these nosy ass people off." He said laughing.

He noticed she didn't join in. When he looked over at her, his heart started to hurt, Tasha was looking out the window crying.

"What's wrong ma? What did I say?"

"It's not you Mako, it's just that what I said at dinner was true. My mother was killed when I was in the second grade."

At that moment Mako and Tasha both realize they really knew very little about the other. They had been messing around for a minute, but now it was no longer fun and games for either of them. Tasha was falling for Mako and he was falling for her.

Mako didn't know what to say, he wanted to know the story behind the murder, but he didn't want to pry. He didn't have to ask though, Tasha began the story that she was told of her mother's murder.

"Oh baby, I didn't know. I am so sorry." Mako said, pulling her close to him as he parked in front of her building.

"Now, I understand why you refuse to leave the hood."

"It's okay, but now that you know something about me, tell me something about you, come upstairs."

As much as Mako wanted to, he knew Abraham was going to tear into his ass if he didn't show up, and if he went upstairs with Tasha tonight, seeing Abraham would definitely be out the question.

"I can't tonight ma, but tomorrow it's just me and you, okay?"

"Alright." Tasha said, not hiding the disappointment in her voice.

On the drive to his grandfather's house Mako thought about the conversation that he had with Tasha. After such a light evening she had hit him with some heavy shit, but that only endeared him to her more. What he would have shared with her that night if he didn't have a prior commitment with his grandfather, was that he too was an orphan. That they were able to feel each other on such a deep and intimate level made him feel like she was his soul mate.

He decided when he pulled into his grandfather's driveway he was going to do something really special for her. He couldn't wait to see her tomorrow. Before he got out of the car, he text her.

Be ready by 10:00. I am taking you to your favorite breakfast spot. So we can start the day right.

He smiled as he thought of how excited she was going to be, he couldn't wait to see the look on her face.

"Pops, where you at?" Mako called through the house looking for his grandfather.

He had let himself in with his house key and made his way to his grandfather's office. Abraham was sitting behind his desk going over some paper work. The only light in the office was from a desk size Tiffany lamp his grandmother had purchased years before he was born. Abraham didn't even look up.

"Macon have a seat."

The pensive tone in his grandfather's voice let Mako know something was definitely up, and he was sure whatever it was connected to tonight's function. Mako was about to speak but was cut off by Abraham.

"I want to tell you a story," Abraham began. Mako had a look on his face like not again and Abraham had to chuckle out loud. "It's not one that you've heard before son. Would you like a drink?"

"Naw, I'm good Pops." Mako declined. "Just get to the story."

Abraham cleared his throat and began to tell Mako the story of Charles Johnson and his best friend Abraham Clark. Abraham told of story of how the two formed a friendship when Abraham met Charlie, broken and bloody in the alley. He went on to tell how the two quickly began running the streets together. With Charles showing Abraham the ropes of surviving in Chicago's ghetto, and Abraham's business mind and southern manners they quickly came of age together and ran the West side.

Macon's mind was blown. Halfway through his grandfather's story he decided maybe he did need a drink. He knew his grandfather had gotten down back in the day, but pimping, bootlegging, all this was new to him. He had a million questions to ask but decided to let Abraham keep speaking. He couldn't help but smile thinking, *I knew Pops was a motherfucking gangsta.*

Seeing the smile across Mako's face made Abraham stop his story for the moment.

"Macon I am not telling you this to inspire you any more than you already are to be in these streets. If you would let me get to the end, you will see why I am telling you this."

Mako nodded in agreement and sipped and listened. Abraham decided to cut it short and get to the point, not wanting to glamorize this lifestyle that had brought him the wealth and power he possessed at that moment.

"So Pops, where is this best friend Charlie at? How come I have never heard you talk about him or seen him around here?"

Abraham knew Macon would ask that question, so he gave him a truthful answer, as truthful as he was willing to be at that moment.

"Charlie's wife had just given birth. We were outside the hospital smoking cigars and congratulating him. He asked me that night to be the godfather to his seed. I was honored, he was my best friend, my brother." Abraham was choked up when he made that statement. "I promised him from that day forward that if anything ever happened to him I would look out for his seed and his wife. Later that day, Charlie was gunned down outside the hospital on his way to see his wife and twin sons."

Twins? Mako was starting to feel a churning in his stomach. Too much of his grandfather's story was starting to fall in place. It was a puzzle that was not going to end with a pretty picture in the end. As much as he didn't want to ask the question, he did. Swallowing the last of his glass of Hennessey in one gulp.

"So Pops, what was the name of these twins, your godsons?" Mako's heart was beating so fast he thought it was going burst out of his chest.

"I think you already know the answer to that Macon." Abraham said, looking him in his eyes and flinging the bag full of shark seals across his desk.

"They are family Macon in more ways than one, now that you are dating their niece. What would she think about you trying to destroy her family's empire? Which by the way is an extension of our family empire?"

Mako was speechless. He had no idea. He had betrayed his grandfather unknowingly and also broke one of the golden rules, we honor all family ties until death with loyalty. Mako felt bad about that, but thought he should be given the benefit of the doubt. He had no idea, his grandfather should have told him about this connection years ago.

"I know what you are thinking Macon. I should have told you years ago about our connection to the Johnson family. That is information on a strictly need to know basis, and I told your hardheaded ass time and time again to stay out these streets. A hard head makes a soft ass, son."

Macon hated being scolded by his grandfather, but he took it out of respect and he knew he deserved it. He just kept thinking about what was going to happen when Tasha found out. She would think everything he felt and did for her was not genuine, and oh shit, he forgot he had to definitely let Timmo know the Altged Garden plan was out. All that shit as out. He knew Tim would be heated, but he didn't have a choice. He couldn't continue to damage family bonds and business connections anymore. He had to grow up.

"I've cleaned up your mess for the last time Macon" Abraham said sternly. Now either you buckle down and get with the program and do your job as my campaign manager, or you can throw it all down the gutter in these pissy streets. The choice is your son."

Abraham had just hit Mako with some really powerful shit. His mind still reeling, he thought about the familial connection that he shared with the very men whose empire he was trying to destroy. Never mind the fact that he was messing around with their niece. Once Abraham had finished his story, Macon knew what it was he needed to do. He had to call Timmo and tell him that phase two of the plan was dead in the water.

He knew Timmo wasn't going to like it, but this is the way it had to be. As far as Mako was concerned the twins were like sons in his grandfather's eyes and if that was so, it made them his uncles. Yes, it was a lot to digest in one sitting, considering all the scheming, plotting, and planning that it had taken to get to this point would be for nothing, but he had implicit instructions from Abraham to cease and desist. That is exactly what he planned on doing. Timmo was just going have to get with the program.

The next morning Mako went ahead with his plans to treat Tasha to a day out. He pulled up outside of her door at 9:30 and text that he was outside waiting. When she came out she looked like her spirits had picked up.

"Okay, I'm hungry let's go."

166

"Alright love!" He said kissing her on the forehead. "I got a quick stop to make before I take you to Lume's."

When they pulled up in front of a travel agency Tasha was confused.

"What are we doing here?"

"Just come I gotta stop here right fast."

When they got inside of Luxurious World Travels, they were greeted by a smiling blond hair, blue eyed girl who directed them to the back. Mako greeted the travel agent with a hug and they proceeded to start their business.

"Oh, my little Macon, I haven't seen you in years. Congratulations on the graduation."

"Thank you Mrs. Williams." Macon said kissing her on the cheek.

"Ok baby," she said handing him a large manila envelope, "the plane tickets, reservation confirmations and everything else you need is in there."

"Plane tickets? You going somewhere?" Tasha inquired, still not sure why they had to stop here before he took her to Lume's.

Damn she was starving for one of those Greek omelets right about now.

Mako laughed as they left the travel agency. "Yes, Tasha WE are going somewhere. How do you feel about Jamaica?"

"Stop playing Mako."

Tasha looked at him seriously. When she saw he was dead serious, she squealed with delight. She was so excited the thoughts of that Greek omelet went right out the window.

"Yeah, I plan on leaving the day after the mayoral election. Once Pops wins, I am definitely due for a nice vacation, and I would rather spend my time with you."

"Good game." Tasha joked.

As they continued to Lume's, the conversation in the car was mostly Tasha talking about shopping, getting her hair done and all the preparations for this trip. She had never been out of the country before and told Mako she didn't have a passport.

"That's okay ma. We can make a quick stop in Miami before we catch our flight to Jamaica they do quick passports in about two hours. We can be ready to see the world."

He was cheesing almost as hard as Tasha. The way he saw her eyes light up with joy and gratitude when he told her they were going to Jamaica made him feel some kind of way.

Pulling up in the parking lot of Lume's got Tasha's stomach to growling. She went to stop Mako before he got out the car.

"Hey, what made you give me such a surprise? I have always wanted to go to Jamaica."

Mako looked Tasha in her eyes as he spoke, "The other night for the first time I saw you truly sad. To see all the life and happiness just dim for a second in your eyes let me know that I wanted to bring the sunshine in your life, and Jamaica has plenty to spare."

Tasha didn't know what to say. His words were so sincere she felt that he truly cared. The only men in her life who had truly cared about her happiness up until that point were her uncles. The words Mako had just spoken convinced Tasha to take a chance on loving a man for the first time in her life.

After breakfast Mako dropped Tasha off at home. He told her he had to catch up with Timmo and he would call her later. After a quick kiss and handing Tasha a wad of cash to start shopping, he went on his way. He hit Timmo on the phone to let him know to meet him at the apartment on Kostner. He didn't know how he was going to tell Timmo that all their illegal operations out south had to cease. The Roseland community was platinum mine when it came to the drug game, and Timmo would not walk away so easily.

Mako knew that the streets were Timmo's bread and butter, so he had always made sure that of their illegal schemes Timmo saw the most profit. For Mako it was about the respect and prestige in the streets, to Timmo it was all about the mighty dollar. Their friendship benefitted them both in achieving their goals. Since they were shorty's they had been wrecking shop together and looking out for one another, but now they were adults and Mako now had different goals.

However, Timmo's goal remained the same to get cash in every part of the city. He knew that with the money, respect and power would come but he didn't care about that. It was just perks to being a street millionaire. Mako had decided to basically buy out his interest in the business. He knew Timmo was about the paper and what he had decided to pay him to walk away was a very nice figure.

They had made a lot of money over the years, and could have made more but up until recently Mako had always tried to be under the radar of his grandfather, and he knew being a multi-million dollar drug dealer would attract way too much attention. They had a made a few million in illegal money over the years and had tricked off a lot of that. Mako had decided to put away childish things and become a man. He realized why his grandfather had wanted him to stay out the streets, and with Tasha now in his life, he saw better things for himself on the horizon.

In Mako's mind, no matter what business was or was not conducted between him and Timmo, they would always remain friends. Once Mako began to run the game down to Tim, he was starting to think his friend might not feel the same way.

"So you mean to tell me that you are about to throw away the biggest hustle we have ever had right now?"

Timmo was furious. He couldn't believe Mako had come up in the spot talking that bullshit about saying fuck the game. He could understand that part. He knew his friend was not cut out for the long run in the streets because he had a nice pile of legal money to always fall back on. Timmo never had that option. The streets were his mother, the game was his daddy and his paper was his bitch. That was all he had ever needed to get by in this world, but with Mako refusing to entertain taking over the Altged Gardens anymore, Timmo was furious.

"T, it ain't that serious. There are other spots to take over in the city. That ain't the only one."

Mako was trying to make light of the situation once he saw how angry Timmo was about the situation. He was cool with Mako bowing out the business ventures, but once he forbid him from taking over the G that is when the discussion got heated.

"Look fam, I understand the situation you got with your granddad. I got mad respect for Old Abe, but I don't eat from his table." Timmo said, looking Mako straight in the eye.

There was a tension, a hostility in the room that was never present before. Something in the dynamic of their friendship shifted at that moment, but neither could put their finger on it.

"As far as you buying your way out of the business, it is unnecessary. You have more than looked out for me and you always have my gratitude, but since our business together is done, the choices I make from here on out to run MY business, is none of your concern fam."

"Tim..."Mako began but was interrupted.

"I hear you fam, the G is off limits, I'll let sleeping dogs lie on the strength that you my peeps and I don't need Old Abe running after me." He joked.

Inside Mako breathed a sigh of relief. As long as he could keep Timmo out of the Gardens, everything would be at peace. It had been a heated debate, but Timmo had never broken his word to Mako especially when it came to business. He just wanted to keep Timmo out of harm's way, knowing nothing good would come of it for either of them.

Before Mako left they blew a blunt together as friends, him leaving the apartment happy that everything had worked out as planned. Timmo had different thoughts. His thoughts were of going through with his plans for taking over the Gardens. He would wait until Mako went on his trip and the election was over. He hated to betray Mako, but he knew that from that day forward their lives were destined for different paths. As he laid his plans down to take over the projects, he drank Remy and smoked blunts to mourn the death of a friendship.

CHAPTER 17

Making Plans

On the other side of town, Tasha was slipping off her shoes and calling Jaleesa to tell her the good news. Jaleesa was excited for Tasha and let her know she had some good news of her own to share, but she would rather do it in person. They made plans to get together after Jaleesa got off work that afternoon to catch up with each other.

"Just to pre-warn you Kristen is coming over here later too."

Jaleesa couldn't help but to suck her teeth. "Whatever, it's your house and your friend. As long as that hooker stays in her lane we're good." What Jaleesa really wanted to say was, "Why you go to kick it with that bitch," but in her mind it sounded just like something Kristen's jealous ass would say.

Tasha laughed it off. "Girl, you're silly. I'll catch you later though sis, I got some shopping to do."

Four hours later, Jaleesa got off the bus in front of the donut shop. The smell of freshly fried donuts made her head for the door to get two buttermilk glazed. They were one of her favorite munchies after blowing with Tasha. Old Fashioned Donuts had been there for fifty years, it was a staple of the Roseland community. People came from all over the city just to get these donuts. Krispy Kreme ain't got shit on that donut shop!

"Umm, let me get two buttermilk glazed and a hot dog and fries." Jaleesa said to the girl behind the counter.

Before she could pay her a voice behind her spoke up, "I got you Leesa."

Jaleesa laughed. "Always Juicy to the rescue for a damsel in distress."

She couldn't help but notice him blush at the compliment. Juicy was so humble, she liked that about him. In high school they'd both been at the top of their class at Whitney Young, and had a friendly competitive rivalry when it came to academics. Every time she beat him at something, she would gloat, yet when he came out on top he never boasted. When he was named valedictorian to her salutatorian for high school graduation he comforted her when she cried in the gym.

He knew how hard she had worked for it, but he had outshone her by a two points on a calculus final they had studied for together. That was the first time he saw Jaleesa as more than a feisty tough chick from Roseland. She was vulnerable and beautiful and all he wanted to do was make her feel that way.

"Juicy are you listening to me?" Jaleesa snapped her fingers in Juicy's face. "Stop all that daydreaming boy."

After Jaleesa got her food, Juicy walked her around the corner. He already knew where she was headed. Posting up on Tasha's porch on some milk crates Jaleesa asked Juicy to roll a blunt while she got her eat on. She wanted to tell Tasha the good news so bad and she was mad she had to wait on her to get back from spending some man's money. As she watched Juicy roll the blunt, she couldn't help but to notice how sexy his lips were.

"What're you looking at?" Juicy asked handing her the blunt.

"Nothing." Jaleesa blushed.

She felt ashamed being caught in the act. Shit that was Juicy, no part of him could be sexy to her right? Quickly trying to change the subject she started.

"I got a letter today from University of Wisconsin at Madison."

With this Juicy's ears perked up. Although Jaleesa had graduated second in her high school class, received a 23 on her ACT, and got accepted to numerous colleges, she decided to put off going to college for a year to work and save money.

She had academic scholarships to many colleges and turned them down. There was something about not succeeding at trying for something you had worked so long and hard for that crushed a little of her spirit. Juicy never understood why or how she could give up so easily. He had also been accepted to many schools of his choice, and had the privilege of attending Morehouse for a year, before he got kicked out for being in the wrong place, at the wrong time. He didn't fair too much better than her, but at least he had the courage to take the chance to dare to rise above this madness.

"So what did it say?" Juicy asked clearing his throat.

"It said that I have been accepted in the education department as a student and I start in January." Jaleesa said, a smile beaming from ear to ear.

Juicy remembered that smile, and so did his heart. He was proud of her more than he would ever allow himself to say.

"That's what's up Leesa!" He said, hiding the emotions in his voice.

This dimmed Jaleesa's smile a bit. She thought of all the people in the world he would be the happiest for her, even more than Tasha who was never really into school. Juicy took all this in and realized that she believed he was envious, or didn't care. He immediately tried to correct his action. He decided that if she had finally found the courage to live up to her potential, he could find the courage to let his emotions show.

"Of all the people in the hood you know how I feel about you rising above this madness. I will never forget the dreams, goals, and accomplishments we shared when we were younger."

For the first time Jaleesa's eyes were being opened up to the true feelings Juicy had for her and she decided to listen.

"I know how hurt and disappointed you were when I was named valedictorian. If I would have known how it would have killed your spirit, I would have failed that test for you."

Jaleesa was caught off guard by the things he was saying and she needed him to stop before he said the wrong thing. She wasn't ready for this. Not now, she was leaving and he was staying. She didn't have time for love games right now, but who said anything about love?

"Juicy..."

"Wait, let me finish." Juicy said firmly.

He had so much more to say, but he could see Jaleesa was hesitant to hear his truth so he edited what he truly intended to say.

"As I was saying, I am going to be the first to congratulate you by taking you out to dinner. Anywhere you want to go."

Jaleesa felt like a fool, she had almost put her foot dead in her mouth. He wasn't going to profess his love, he was going to take her out to dinner and congratulate her on her accomplishments, like he had always done in the past.

"You don't have to do that," she said. "I know you, of all people want this for me."

"Well at least let me feed you."

Before Jaleesa could get out her reply Tasha and Kristen pulled up in front of the house.

"Hey Boo!" Tasha said, jumping out of the car excited to share the news of her Jamaica trip with Jaleesa.

Jaleesa was relieved that Tasha had spared her form a very awkward moment, but she had decided that she would take Juicy up on his offer of dinner. After all, what was a dinner amongst friends?

"Juicy why you standing there? Help me get these bags out the car." Tasha demanded, as she began handing him bags to take upstairs for her. Juicy laughed and shook his head.

"Where are you coming from T, or should I ask where you going with all these bags?" Jaleesa joked.

"You won't believe me when I tell you. Mako asked me to go to Jamaica with him after the election bitch!" Tasha squealed.

"Stop playing." Jaleesa and Kristen said at the same time.

Jaleesa was shocked and excited for her friend, Kristen was shocked and jealous. All the moves she was making with Timmo and the only time they went out of town was we he needed her to deliver packages. Quickly swallowing her envy Kristen congratulated Tasha.

"Girl I heard they got some fire ass weed for the low in Jamaica. Smoke some for me." Kristen said.

"Alright, I see y'all got a lot to talk about." Juicy said, excusing himself as he came out of the hallway from depositing Tasha's bags.

"Think about what I said." He told Jaleesa before walking off.

She wanted to tell him her answer but she didn't want the girls to think it was a date. She didn't feel like talking about her feelings for

Juicy and definitely didn't want Kristen all up in her demo so she nodded her head and let him walk away.

"What was that all about?" Tasha asked.

"Nunya." Jaleesa laughed, as the three women went upstairs.

"So now that you know my good news, what you got to tell me?" Tasha asked Jaleesa while rolling a blunt.

Jaleesa didn't know how to tell T they were parting ways so she just spit it out, "I am leaving in January to go to school at UWM."

Tasha almost chocked on the smoke. "So you finally decided to leave and do what you were meant to do?"

Jaleesa was puzzled she had thought Tasha would take it much harder than that. They had been inseparable since birth after all.

"Look Le Le, you were always the smart one, hell you are the reason I made it to high school graduation. I expected you to leave me after high school, but you stayed. I never understood why, but I am sure you had your reasons."

Tasha knew the reason she just didn't want Kristen to see a more vulnerable side of her best friend.

"Well you better hit this blunt cause before you leave that shit is coming to an end I'm sure." She said passing the blunt to Jaleesa.

Kristen was irritated with the love she felt coming from Tasha towards Jaleesa, and knowing she had her own good news to share quickly interrupted the moment.

"Well, I've got to tell you I'm leaving you too Tasha" Kristen said.

Seeing Tasha was puzzled, Kristen told them how Timmo had copped her a crib on the low-end and she was officially moving out the hundreds for good.

"Good for you Krissy. I knew you would graduate to a real baller one day." Tasha joked, taking the blunt from Kristen.

Although it was meant as a joke Kristen felt slighted by Tasha's remark. Now that she had finally made a come up, this bitch hated.

"I'll smoke to that!" Seconded Jaleesa.

Irritated to the point of no return, Kristen wanted to shout in Tasha's face how fucking dumb she was for fucking a nigga who was out to take all the cash that had her living in luxury throughout her life. Instead, she swallowed it once again, looked at her phone.

"Oh y'all, I got to ride. I am supposed to be hooking up with my boo later. Deuces." And with that Kristen walked out the door

"What's up with that bitch?" Jaleesa inquired.

"I have no idea. I just know she's been acting real funny lately." Tasha said. "The bitch will be alright. I'm going to Jamaica and no one can steal that sunshine right now."

For the rest of the night Tasha and Jaleesa talked, smoked and reminisced about their lives together and the past dreams and future goals. While Tasha talked of becoming the wife of a political legacy in the city, Jaleesa talked about opening her own charter school in the hood one day. Before they both passed out that night in Tasha's bed, they promised that no matter where their lives took them, they would always be sisters.

"The ties that bind us, will bind us together forever sister." Tasha mumbled before they drifted into a deep sleep.

The election was three days away and both Abraham and Macon had been busy making rounds in neighborhoods where the majority of voters were black. Abraham knew that black people would come out to vote if the candidate was black. So he campaigned hard on the Southside of Chicago, where the nation's largest concentration of black folks lived. He promised everything from affordable grocery stores, to new schools, and renovated parks.

Mako thought it would be a good idea for Tasha to tag along with him. He knew that the people on the Southside knew who her uncles were and that might carry a little weight in the polls. He had even enlisted Juicy and Jaleesa to go to the train station at 95th and register people to vote. They were all working to get Abraham in office, and for the first time Mako felt good about an accomplishment he made in the legitimate world.

The night of the election WGN announced Abraham had won by a margin of three percent, being mostly compromised of new, young black voters. Juicy, Jaleesa, Tasha and Mako all celebrated at the campaign headquarters in K-town with Abraham. Bottles of expensive champagne were popped, business deals were cemented, and Abraham had reached the pinnacle of his life. He had achieved a feat they said no black man would after Mayor Harold Washington.

Abraham had played his cards right for over three decades and now his dreams were coming to fruition, he just wished his son and his wife were there to witness it. After they had announced his victory, he met eyes with Terry first. With a firm nod he cemented Terry's comfortable place as the king of Chicago's underworld. With Abraham at the helm politically, Terry could not and would not be touched. It was a victory for them both.

"Congrats Pops!" Mako greeted his grandfather with a firm handshake and a hug. "The legacy lives on."

"Thank you son, you more than did your part, this is not just my victory, but a victory for the Clark family."

Mako knew family included his grandmother, and parents who weren't there to share this moment. The party went on for a while, but Mako knew he had an early flight in the morning with Tasha, so they said their goodbyes and slipped out. Jaleesa and Juicy decided to stay, they were actually having a good time, enjoying the thanks they were getting for helping out at the last minute. Knowing Tasha would be leaving in the morning Jaleesa gave her a big hug and told her to have fun. Mako gave Juicy dap, and thanked him again for helping out, and the couples went their separate ways.

Needless to say Timmo was not happy with Mako deciding to forego their plans of invading the G. He had love for Mako, but that nigga was playing with his money, so as far as Timmo was concerned all bets were off. Knowing that his friend was going to Jamaica with his bitch had been the devil's way of showing Timmo to go for the gusto. He knew with him being out of town, it would keep Mako in the clear with Abraham, and him to. That old dude was one person he was actually scared to go to war with. Abraham was a real OG.

So while they were out west celebrating, Timmo, Amir and Booman were celebrating too. Tomorrow night they planned to run up in blocks two, nine, and twelve in the Gardens. These were the blocks were the twins most lucrative weed, crack, and dope houses were located. They had almost forty soldiers that were well trained and ready to eat. Timmo knew the twins were still hurting from the Roseland caper and he was betting, more like hoping they weren't ready to go to war, but if they did, he had a backup plan.

A plan only he knew. He planned on including Amir and Booman in on plan B, but it was strictly on a need to know basis, and they didn't need to know yet. Timmo expected there to be a bloodbath that is what he wanted. Leave no one alive at any spot was the number one rule. He didn't care about leaving witnesses he just wanted to make a statement to the twins that he was not scared to leave a barrage of bodies in his wake. If plan A didn't bring the twins to their knees, plan B would definitely lay them down.

With the election being tonight, and Timmo having secured his firepower and army, nothing was stopping him from running up in that bitch tomorrow night, not even Jesus Christ himself. C.R.E.A.M had always been his motto, and just because his homie wasn't riding with him, didn't mean he wasn't gonna ride. Timmo was hungry and he would let nothing get in the way of his meal.

While Timmo, Booman and Amir were plotting downstairs, Kristen was upstairs in her and Timmo's room contemplating. She knew about plan B, she was a major player in it. She would have to cross a line and burn a bridge, and by burning that bridge she might alienate the only person in the world who truly loved her, Samantha. Kristen tried to blow those thoughts out of her mind by blowing a blunt of Kush. After a few minutes, it had kicked in and she found herself daydreaming about all the shit she always wanted and was now going to have.

Tasha had always clowned her about fucking with low-budget ass niggas.

"You need to find a nigga with some GO and not some GIVE." She used to say to her all the time.

Kristen chuckled to herself as she thought that the nigga she had now, had more GO than she could ever imagine, and she planned on going all the way with him, if that's what it took. Still, she couldn't help hoping there would be no need for plan B.

CHAPTER 18

No Turning Back

When Tasha and Mako got off the plane in Jamaica, the first thing that greeted them was the humidity and all the sounds, sights, and smells of a culture founded by people who were once slaves. Tasha was assaulted by the beauty of the island, she took so many pictures in that first day, and she decided she might need another memory card for her camera. Mako just enjoyed the look of excitement and pleasure on her face as they tried new food, dances, and rum cocktails.

There first night there, they made love on the private beach attached to the villa Mako had rented for the week. He wanted to show Tasha another side of the game and another side of himself. He dedicated every minute to her, so much that on day three when his phone was ringing off the hook from a number he didn't know, he cut it off. It was just going to be him and her these next few days, he was in love for the first time and he wanted to relish in his happiness.

Later on, back in the Chi...

"Okay Cortez, you ready to earned your stripes." Amir said passing the blunt to the minor.

Little Cortez was nervous all he could do was nod his head as he hit the blunt. He didn't want to say the wrong thing and loose his position, but he'd never committed a murder and he knew that murder was his mission for the night. Amir knew shorty was green on the murder books, but all it took was the first time and it was like pie afterward. Amir had caught his first murder at thirteen, a robbery gone wrong. The only reason he didn't get caught is because he had robbed a known drug dealer and the cops saw it as someone taking out the trash for them. That was one of the other reasons that he only robbed drug dealers when he was sticking niggas up. Police don't give a shit about a nigga in the hood losing his life.

"Okay with the fucking pep talk." Timmo said agitated. "Look little nigga, either you want to get this paper or not. Time for talking is over." With that he cock his gun and gave the signal. It was time to go to war.

Pulling up in the lot of block two, Little Cortez got out to knock on the door of the weed spot. If he would have not been so nervous or paying more attention, maybe he would have noticed how deserted the lot was on a Friday night.

"Who dat?" A voice from the other side of the door called out.

"Let me get five bags of that gristle." Cortez answered.

Hearing the door unlock made his adrenaline rush. He knew the next few second would determine the outcome of his future.

"Can I get five for forty?" Cortez asked as he stepped slightly in the doorway. When he walked in he did a quick scan of the room. It seemed quiet upstairs and all he could hear was the TV the man was watching. When the dealer went to reach in his Crown Royal bag for the weed, Cortez pulled out his Desert Eagle. The man looked up when he heard the gun cock and almost shitted on himself.

When he looked in the kids eyes he didn't see a killer, he saw a little nigga trying to come up, so he decided to plead for his life.

"Hey shorty, you can have the weed and the dough, my life is worth more." He said, thinking about how his two year old son and baby mother were asleep upstairs.

"You're right, it is. Worth millions more."

Within the span of two seconds, Little Cortez had become a killer. The only thing that shook him from the excitement, regret and adrenaline he was feeling were the sudden screams of a child. Being new to this murder game he wasn't gonna kill no babies, he was sure Timmo didn't want that. As Cortez ran from the scene of the crime, leaving the money and work as he had been instructed. All of sudden, he heard what to some would sound like a 4THof July fireworks show, but he knew better, he knew it was the sound of war.

Things might have gone as planned in block two, but in blocks nine, and twelve things weren't going as well. Word spreads fast in the Altged Gardens among the blocks, and what had went down in block two was spreading before it was finished happening. Unbeknownst to Timmo, the twins had assumed that whoever had hit their Roseland spots would be hitting the G next. They had warned their workers well in advance to be aware, so when the weed man's baby momma found him dead on their couch, she called Al-G before she called the ambulance.

Back in block nine...

The BD's were ready for them. They came out in full force refusing to share their turf with any nigga not from the G, especially some West side niggas. There was so much shooting, the innocents stayed on the floors and in the bathtub of their apartments for thirty full minutes. This was the Chi after all, it was mostly innocent people that got killed when shit like this went down, and no one wanted to be a victim that night. Eleven people were injured that night in block nine. Two were left dead and they were both under the age of thirteen.

In block twelve, Amir and Booman were under heavy fire. It seemed like niggas just start coming out of the woodworks, they weren't expecting to have to fight this many niggas tonight. It seemed like random friendlies were out protecting this piece of shit project.

"Where the fuck is that nigga Timmo?" Booman said aloud.

184

"Fuck that nigga, I'm finna get the fuck out of here. Man we about to lose this fucking war. Shit!" Amir cursed as he saw all the money that could have been gained being washed away in a river of blood. "Come on cuz." He said grabbing Booman.

Somehow Amir and Booman were able to duck and dodge the gunfire and safely make it out of the G and on to the E-way. From there Amir called Timmo, he called him for thirty minutes before he finally got an answer.

"Where you at nigga?" Amir said urgently when Timmo picked up.

"I just got the fuck out of there?" Timmo lied.

He hadn't been stupid enough to stick around the battle, he was a general. He directed the war, he didn't fight it. He was hoping that fate would have cut Amir and Booman a raw deal with death. That way he wouldn't have to deal with cutting them out the picture later.

"Where you at? I'm going to come scoop you."

"Man, we on Doty Rd. coming from the G. Hurry up nigga I don't want to get hit by a fucking car. I just escaped death."

"Man the shit wasn't supposed to go down like that." Booman said. "I thought the shit was supposed to be easy as pie. All this shit for nothing."

Booman shook his head. The flashing of headlights let them know Timmo was approaching. As soon as they hopped in the car Amir proceeded to tell him what went down.

"Fuck! Fuck! Fuck!" Was all Timmo could say as he puffed on his blunt.

This shit was not supposed to happen like this. Out of almost forty soldiers, they had lost fifteen. Some were shot and some were beaten to death by the members of the family they had tried to take over. The more Timmo thought about it, the more he began to believe Mako had set him up for the okey doke.

They had known each other since childhood and Mako knew Timmo couldn't resist the temptation. That is why he had warned him away from the Gardens, because he had snitched himself out to the twins.

"That dumb ass nigga!" He said out loud.

"Who?" Amir and Booman said in unison, thinking he was referring to either of them.

Timmo was pissed and chose not to answer either one of them.

"Kristen!" He called. "Come downstairs!" Kristen's stomach was turning. She had heard their loud conversation downstairs and knew things didn't go as planned. She was hoping to stay out of it, so that she could feign innocence if she needed to later, but she knew by the way Timmo called her name that would not be happening. It was time for plan B and she was the main player.

When Kristen got down stairs, Timmo informed his crew that it was not all lost. When he told them about plan B Amir was pissed.

"We should have made that plan A in the first place, then we wouldn't be covered in the blood of our soldiers." He snarled, his eyes piercing Timmo.

It was at that moment Amir realized Timmo didn't have a drop of blood anywhere on him. To just leave the bloodbath they had come from and not have one drop on him wasn't sitting right with Amir. He went to speak on it but a voice in his had told him to hold his tongue, and he listened.

186

"Look, all that don't matter now." Timmo said staring at Amir with the same intensity he had shown. "I refuse to walk away with nothing and this way we can get what we came for. Just a different way."

Amir and Booman couldn't argue with that, too much had been lost to walk away with nothing if they could just have a little piece of the pie, they could go their separate ways until the heat died down in the city. Maybe set up shop somewhere else. It sounded good to Booman's ears, but Amir wasn't buying it. He shook his head and agreed with Timmo, but he knew this nigga had planned to snake him and Booman out since the beginning. He just hope his cousin wasn't too dumb to see through his game, but by the look on Booman's face as he drank in every word Timmo said, Amir knew his cousin was too far gone in the bullshit to see the truth. Timmo never planned to share any of the big money with them, they were loose ends that he would eventually need to tie up. Amir didn't know about Booman, but he knew he would be careful around Timmo's snake ass, and he definitely had to get Timmo before he got him.

"It's okay to turn your phone on you know." Tasha said rubbing Mako's shoulders. They had been in Jamaica for five days and he hadn't answered his phone once. She appreciated all the attention and affection he had showered her with, but she also knew he had a lot of business at home that he should be taking care of. After reassuring him for the third time, he decided to turn his phone on and call his grandfather and check in with him. When Mako turned his phone on, the screen was instantly flooded with a barrage of messages text and voicemail.

"Damn they must really miss us." He joked.

Seeing his grandfather's number so many times, and his uncle terry's had him worried. He walked out on the balcony to call his grandfather. After getting no answer at his office, home or on his cell, he called his Uncle Terry. Seeing as how Mako was on his phone, Tasha decided to turn hers on and call Jaleesa and tell her how great

Jamaica was, but after getting voicemail, she left her a text instead. She was just about to call Kristen when she heard Mako raise his voice on the patio as he closed the door.

What is that about, she wondered, as she put on her headphones taking the door closing as a clue it was a private conversation. As much as she wanted to be nosey, she knew with a man of his caliber, he had to know he could trust the woman he was with. She was just letting him know he could always trust her.

"Uncle Terry, I swear I had nothing to do with that! I told Timmo not to go through with it. He's so fucking hard headed!" Mako said furiously.

He couldn't believe he had taken Timmo at his word, and he had blatantly betrayed him. He knew something like this was bound to happen, that is why he told him to stay away. He was trying to protect him.

"Macon, that isn't the worst of it." Terry started. "Not only did they start a war in the Gardens, they kidnapped Raymond and Charles' niece Jaleesa."

"What?" Macon said it so loud Tasha took her head phones off to hear what she could through the closed door.

"Man Uncle T, that is not even their niece, Tasha is."

"You think I don't know that youngster, you forgot who you are talking to, but you need to be on the first thing flying back this way ASAP. This shit could be a replay of the war that was started with Jackie's death."

"Who is Jackie?"

Realizing he had spoken too much and all that was irrelevant, Terry rushed him home and hung up the phone. Tasha waited for

Mako to come back in, when she heard her name and the word niece, she knew something was up, and the look on Mako's face made her heart sink. Before he could get the full story out Tasha was up and packing.

"Not my sister, Mako I don't understand? What is this about?"

Mako wasn't ready to explain the full story to her just yet, so instead he took her in his arms and let her cry all the way back to the Chi.

When they landed at O'Hare, Tasha's eyes were red and puffy and she was ready to get home to the safety of her uncles. When they got off the plane they were greeted at the gate by two unlikely characters. Al-G and Uncle Terry. When Tasha saw Al-G waiting for her at the gate, she started a fresh round of tears. She was confused what was he doing here, how did he know this is where she was.

She opened her mouth to ask what was going on and Al stopped her.

"Let's get you safe baby girl and then we can talk."

Tasha close her mouth and allowed herself to be led to the car. There was complete silence on the way to their destination wherever that was and she ended up falling asleep on the drive. When she opened her eyes, she saw that they were at Abraham's estate. This was definitely getting more confusing and frustrating by the minute.

"Will someone please tell me what is happening? What's going on where is Le Le."

No one in the car wanted to answer the questions she was asking. It was all so complicated they didn't know where to begin. Looking around the car at these gangsta ass niggas looking at her like they were scared to say something made her want to slap the shit out of all of them.

"Somebody fucking say something or I am going to find my sister myself!"

The look in her eyes was one of hurt, confusion, and determination. The only one who knew that look was Al-G. He knew her since she was a child and she was used to having her way. He just didn't have it in him to break her heart with the truth. He looked at Terry, who gave him a nod.

"I think Macon deserves to tell you he whole truth and nothing but the truth."

Al-G gave him a look that said if he left anything out he would fuck him up. Then the two men got out of the car leaving Mako alone with Tasha and those eyes glaring right through him.

"Baby please say something." She pleaded.

Seeing the hurt in her eyes and knowing he would only cause more, broke his heart. He loved this woman and this was the last thing he had in mind happening. He figured if she loved him like he thought, she would understand that this wasn't his fault somehow. He would make it right, whatever it took, he would do it.

He took a deep breath and began to tell his side of the story. When he had finished, Tasha had slapped him so hard, he saw stars.

"Stay the fuck away from me!" She spat. "You used me, to help destroy my family, and I thought you were…You know what if Jaleesa doesn't come back to me unharmed, you don't have to worry about my uncles killing you. I will do it myself!"

The look in her eyes let him know she was for real. After she slammed the door, he hung his head in shame.

Tasha walked into Abraham's house like she had bought the place. When she came to the room that was full of faces she recognized from her families crew, as well as those she didn't she knew shit was real. She ran straight to the arms of her uncles and they were overjoyed to know she was safe. Abraham had been more than willing to provide proof that his family had nothing to do with the fuckery going down. Since Tasha had ran off with Mako without letting either of her uncles know, they assumed she had met her worse fate.

Deciding to pay Abraham an unfriendly visit, they were welcomed at his door by armed goons. Abraham had heard what had gone down and knew he would be implicated. He just wanted a chance to prove he was free and clear. The twins were his godsons, his family and he had given his word to stay out of their territory. He knew both Macon and Tasha were safe in Jamaica, but when Macon didn't answer his calls, the twins refused to leave until he returned in the next few days. If he hadn't returned with Tasha, Abraham was sure to have a short lived stint as mayor.

Now that she was safe, a burden had been lifted off their minds. Not only had they been waiting for Tasha, they had been waiting for Mako, he was the final piece to this puzzle. They knew who had Jaleesa, but they could not find them. The same niggas that ran up in their shit in Roseland and the Gardens had snatched their niece and were holding her for a three million dollar ransom. Raymond hated to call Lena and tell her what had happened to her daughter, so instead he went to her home to tell her in person.

When Lena answered the door, Raymond was taken away by her beauty. Seeing Raymond at the door startle her, she had a bad feeling about it. The only reason he came all the way over there was to be the bearer of bad news. When he said what he had come to say, Lena began screaming and hitting him over and over. Telling him it was his fault.

"They took my baby." Lena wept over and over.

"Raymond, you promised you would protect her when she was out there. You promised me. You promised me I wouldn't have to worry about this shit invading my life. This is why I left the neighborhood. All the death, drugs, destruction, the shit that killed my best friend, my sister is threatening to take the life of my baby. Why Ray?" She asked with tears in her eyes.

Raymond couldn't answer Lena even if he wanted to, there was a lump in his throat the size of a baseball. He knew he was to blame, at least partially, after Jackie's death he paid Lena's way out the hood and supported her in many ways and for many reasons. He couldn't let her suffer the same fate as his sister, one of their children deserved to grow up with a mother. Although he didn't want her to go, he helped her to walk away.

He knew that by letting her go, he wouldn't be able to see the one person that kept him striving for more, his daughter Jaleesa. No one but Raymond and Lena knew the truth. Raymond figured Charles knew, but it had to be a twin thing because he had never told him until this morning.

"I already knew that." Were the only words Charles spoke.

To think these fools had accidentally taken the thing that meant the most to him. Thinking Jaleesa was his niece and not his daughter, not that it would have made a difference.

The longer Lena cried, the angrier Raymond became. He told her to pack up some things and come with him. He didn't think it was safe for her to be alone right now and she agreed. On the drive to Raymond's house Lena squeezed his hand.

"Just promise me you'll get our baby back Raymond."

"I promise." He said as a single tear rolled down his cheek.

CHAPTER 19

Aftermath

Kristen was nervous as hell, for two days Timmo, Booman, and Amir had Jaleesa locked in the basement. She was their plan B. When Timmo had found out that her uncle was Raymond, he knew that he would need that piece of information at a later date, and this was the later date. He knew the rumors that her mother had died because of the twins' carelessness. He knew that they would pay dearly for her life. Up until today, they had been lenient with her. He knew Kristen might start feeling some type of way if he roughed her up, so he kept his hands to himself. Besides as long as the twins paid, he had no intention on killing her.

She didn't know who they were and hadn't seen their faces. So right now she wasn't a threat, but Timmo had been antsy because the twins were taking longer than expected to get the ransom money together. He had given them an extra hour to get the shit together. The longer he kept the hostage the worst the odds of anyone making it out alive, and he had no plans of meeting his demise before he had a chance to spend that Guap.

The only person she had seen and knew was in on it was Kristen. Kristen had set her up to be snatched by these two under the ruse of walking with her to Pepe's on State to pick up a food order. It took a lot of being fake and phony to pull her off the porch with Juicy that day, but the blunt and the apologies for always being a bitch seemed to help a little bit. Little did she know, Jaleesa was in a good mood because she had finally had that day with Juicy and something was happening between them. She didn't know what, but it felt good and she was going to hold on to that feeling for as long as she could, or at least until January.

While Jaleesa sat outside smoking the blunt, Kristen went in to get her food that she never really ordered. Making sure her back was turned to the window, she gave Amir the call that Jaleesa was outside. Just as Jaleesa bent down to put the blunt out, she was snatched by two masked men. Kristen walked out of Pepe's with two enchiladas, a tostada and some steak tacos for her and her boo. As Timmo pulled up she hopped into the car and they rode off to meet the others on the low end.

"Did you feed her yet?" Timmo asked throwing his keys on the kitchen counter.

"I don't know, I told Amir to do it, she knows me and I don't want to give myself away." Kristen replied.

"Well keep you fucking mouth shut when you feed her. How hard is that?" Timmo said harshly.

Kristen just rolled her eyes and went back upstairs to smoke another blunt. She was trying to stay as far from that shit as possible, even though she was already neck deep.

"Wake up bitch!"

Jaleesa moaned in pain as ice cold water was thrown on her naked, lacerated skin. It felt like Chinese torture. She couldn't tell what time it was, what day it was, or where she was. She could barely remember how she'd gotten to this place. She'd been drugged and kidnaped by two thugs who kept insisting she knew where her best friend Tasha's uncles Raymond and Charles could be found.

It was confusing to say the least; in the beginning they kept insisting she was someone who she was not, her best friend, Tasha. They had bound her hands, feet and mouth with duct tape, and she was tied to a dining room chair in what seemed like someone's basement that had been dry walled and apparently sound proofed to her chagrin. Jaleesa's face felt like it was on fire. The pain in her left eye had become unbearable. It had begun to swell from the butt of the gun to the side of her face, for spitting in one of the gun men's faces, hence the duct tape on her mouth.

"Yo, take the tape off her mouth." The taller of the masked men said to the other.

"Now look shorty, I'm only going to ask you one more time where your Uncle Raymond is." He said menacingly. "The time for games is over. You still got a chance to live little mama, you haven't seen either of our faces, just say the address and we'll let you go. Hell, we'll even drop you off at a hospital."

As the shortest of the pair reached out and snatched the tape from Jaleesa's mouth, she considered making up any address just to get away from this torture. She had no idea where the twins laid their head and was relieved at this point that she didn't. She would have broken hours ago if she did, and she knew that. The thought saddened her, because the twins were like her uncles, just not blood related. A vicious slap to the face shook Jaleesa out of her reflection.

"Shorty are you gonna answer, or is this the end of the line for you? Think long and hard before you answer, these might just be your last words."

When Jaleesa looked into the soulless eyes boring into her from the other side of that mask, she knew that she had no chance in hell of ever leaving this place alive, whether she'd seen their faces or not. A quick prayer raced through her mind and as a tear fell down her face, she thought they may have broken her body, but they wouldn't break the loyalty she had to the Johnson family. For decades, they had held her family down and vice versa, she could never betray them. If she died tonight, she knew Raymond and Charles would kill whoever had done this to her. Although she wanted to survive this situation, the odds were not in her favor, so she answered accordingly.

"Even if I did know where they were, I would never tell you, but I will tell you this, the twins are going to slaughter you and your friend. You will have to live in fear every minute, of every day of your recently shortened lives. Fuck you!"

The taller of the two took his mask off, much to the objection of the shorter man. "What you doing man, don't let her see your face!" He said nervously.

When the taller of the two pulled his mask off Jaleesa felt urine running down her leg. She knew this was the end of the road for her. She knew this nigga, had kicked it with this nigga, and now he came to kill her. She had been set up for the dummy. The devilish smile on the gunman's face said it all.

"Goodnight bitch!" He said with so much venom you knew he had a personal vendetta against her. With that he pulled the trigger.

As Jaleesa was enveloped in darkness, her last thoughts were, "That bitch Kristen..."

****

Timmo's phone rang, when he saw who it was on the caller ID he smiled a little and answered the phone.

"What up Jo?"

"Cut the bullshit Tim, I know what went down while I was gone." Mako said heated. "I told yo ass to stay out of that motherfucker, but you just refused to listen."

Timmo stayed quiet, he didn't want to give too much away, he wanted to know just how much Mako knew, or suspected.

"What you mean Jo, I ain't doing shit?" Timmo played innocent

"Come on man with that bullshit I know you ran up in the G and started a fucking war with my peeps. I asked you to stay out fam and you betrayed me."

Timmo quickly got on twenty from Mako's last statement.

"Betrayed? Nigga you betrayed me. You turned your back on me you told them niggas we was coming and my crew paid the fucking price." Timmo spat.

Knowing that he and his former friend were past forgiveness Mako cut to the chase.

"You got the wrong girl."

Timmo was caught off guard but quickly caught himself.

"I don't know what the fuck you talking about Jo."

"I think you do and Jaleesa is not the twins' niece, Tasha is."

Timmo was so mad, he broke his iPhone by throwing it against the wall.

"What the fuck?" Kristen screamed coming downstairs. "What are you..."

Before she could get the words out Timmo's hands were around her neck squeezing the life out of her.

"Bitch you knew all along she wasn't their niece."

Kristen tried to speak and explain herself but she felt herself fading into blackness. When Kristen came to, she found that she could barely talk and he head was spinning. Timmo was sitting in a chair across from the bed. He had been waiting for her to wake up. He wanted answers and he knew killing her wouldn't get them. Besides he had a little love for Kristen, she had betrayed everyone she knew and loved for him. He at least owed her the chance to explain herself.

When he saw her open her eyes he began.

"So could you tell me why we have Jaleesa in the basement, when you knew all along she wasn't the twins' true niece?"

At this point Timmo's nerves were on edge and he had very little patience for bullshit right now. He had love for Kristen, but that wouldn't stop him from killing her if she didn't tell the truth.

"She is their niece" She started.

"Stop fucking lying Kris! Mako just called and told me Tasha is their niece!" He said rising up out the chair.

Kristen was terrified she had never seen Timmo as angry as he was now.

"She is, she is!" Kristen pled shaking her head. "You heard him refer to her as his niece and she did the same right?"

"Yeah, but what is this shit about Tasha?" He asked

"Let me explain." Kristen began. By the time she was finished talking, Timmo knew everything about Jackie being killed, the war that ensued, and how the twins took Jaleesa under their wing because Lena and Jackie had been the best of friends.

"So you see baby, they will pay the ransom for Jaleesa, out of guilt they feel like they owe Tasha's mom Jackie, and they would protect Jaleesa at all cost."

"Well the cost is three million dollars and them niggas is bullshitting!" Timmo exploded. "Those niggas ain't called back yet!"

"Maybe they have, but your phone is destroyed." Kristen said reminding him that he had broken his phone earlier.

Timmo ran downstairs to retrieve the SIM card from his broken phone. He then took out the SIM card and Kristen's phone and inserted his. The screen instantly lit up with missed calls from the twins. He dialed back immediately.

"So I hope you got my paper, because this bitch ain't too much longer in this world." Timmo said.

"I got the money. Where do you want to meet? Raymond asked.

After they set up where the drop off and pick up would be, Timmo spirits instantly lifted. Kristen had come through for him and he felt kind of bad about choking the shit out of her, but at least next time she would know not to lie to him.

"Amir!" Timmo called as he ran down the stairs. "You ready to get this money Jo?"

"For sure." He answered.

"Alright this is how it is going down."

Timmo told Amir that he would be going to pick up the ransom money. At first Amir thought about it being a set up, but he would rather pick up the money than let Timmo. He didn't trust that nigga out of his sight, so he agreed to pick up the cash. Booman and Timmo would stay with Jaleesa and make sure she didn't escape. As an afterthought he told Kristen to ride with Amir to watch his back and make him less suspicious. No one wanted to be caught with three million unanswered for dollars by the Chicago police. It was almost a given the money and their bodies would disappear.

While Timmo's team on the low end began making moves, Abraham's house was buzzing with activity too.

"So what did he say when you told him Jaleesa wasn't our niece?" Charles asked.

Mako shook his head, "The nigga tried to act like he didn't know what I was talking about, but he knew, he knew."

Since the twins knew Tasha was safe, they had sent away the majority of their goons. Told them to hit the streets and find out where that nigga Timmo was ASAP. Raymond put a one hundred thousand dollar price on Timmo's head and anyone else involved. That would be motivation for any man to find these clown ass niggas. Anyone on the south side, who was connected, knew about the kidnapping and the reward. Besides, Abraham had used his newly gained political connections to pull images off the cameras at the corner of 11th and State Street to get the license plate off the car that was driven in the kidnapping.

What they came up with were temporary tags registered to a woman by the name of Kareema Ray.

Kareema had Beyoncé's *Dance for You* turned up as she packed the last of her dishes. Booman had gotten them a crib out in Riverdale and Kareema couldn't wait to move. Yeah she loved it over east, she had grown up out there but she would take a four bedroom home over apartment living any day, and with little Jason growing up so fast, she was excited that he would have his own backyard to play in and not have to worry about being shot in a city park.

She could not believe her good fortune. Booman had done a complete turnaround. He was spending more time with Jason and buying them anything their heart desired. Kareema knew he was still out there tricking off, especially at the damn strip club, but it didn't matter because for the first time in forever, he came home most nights, and that home was with her and Jason. That meant more to her than anything he bought her. While Kareema was upstairs packing, Al-G and Terry were lurking.

"It says she stays on the third floor in 3-E." Al-G said "Now how are we gonna get in the building?"

"Follow me."

The men got out the car and Terry began ringing random bells in the building. Someone eventually buzzed them in without even asking who it was. They walked straight upstairs to Kareem's apartment where they heard Beyoncé playing loudly outside the door. Terry pulled something out of his pocket and began picking the lock. Al-G looked somewhat surprised.

"What?" Terry questioned. "It's a skill a man never forgets."

The two men opened the door and quickly scanned the apartment. They hadn't seen the car outside so they were just coming to see what they could find here. They weren't expecting the kidnappers to be home, but someone was.

"Tonight I'm gonna dance for you." Kareem sang at the top of her lungs, as she gyrated her way across the kitchen, sealing the last of the boxes.

When she turned around and saw two men in black masks, she dropped the box of dishes and screamed. Terry quickly grabbed her and put his hand around her mouth.

"Bitch shut the fuck up and tell us where yo bitch ass baby daddy at!" Al-G spat.

Kareem knew this was too good to be true. She had never seen Booman with so much steady money, she should have known his ass was up to no good to get it. Thinking about how much she wanted to live to see her son again, she pointed them to the money Booman had stashed in the apartment.

"We didn't come for the money, we came for the girl."

"What girl?" Kareema asked confused. "That bitch ass nigga! Y'all over her because of some random ass bitch he fucking with? I don't know shit about her or what the fuck he been doing in those streets."

The two men looked at each other trying to gauge her honesty.

"I swear to God, I don't know what y'all talking about. All I know is that Booman said he was going to kick it on the low-end tonight. That's all I know, now please just take the money and let me go. I don't have anything to do with this." She cried.

Fortunately for Kareema, the two men believed her. Terry threw her down on the kitchen floor, taking her cell phone off the table on their way out. When they left Kareema cried and sobbed, she had almost lost her life over some bullshit Booman had brought to her door. What if the baby would've been there? That was it for Kareema, she picked the stacks of money off the floor and put them in Booman's old backpack.

She packed up a few things of little man's and called a cab to her sister's house where he was spending the night. She had decided that she would run off with the fifty thousand dollars and make a new life for herself and her son. It was a wrap for her and big Jason, but her and little man had a bright future ahead of him in the morning.

"The low end. That's where that nigga at somewhere on the low." Terry hung up his call with Abraham.

After relaying the message about Booman's whereabouts Abraham had them pull up police cameras from the low end trying to find that Lexus. Within a half hour they had a hit. The car was parked on the street in front of a restored two flat on 35th and King Drive. They didn't know what to expect when they made their way to the apartment building.

They had sent Raymond out with the money, just to make sure that the kidnappers thought everything was going as planned. In the meanwhile, teams of goons were pulling closer to the house where Jaleesa was being kept ready to lay anything down in their path.

"Okay Kristen you stay in the car and I will go around the corner to get the money. Keep it running because we're peeling the fuck out ASAP." Amir told her before getting out the car.

Kristen was nervous and her hands were shaking as she tightly gripped the steering wheel. Up until this point she was able to hide her part in the scheme, but she knew that Tasha would eventually put two and two together and realized she played a larger role in the whole scheme. She hadn't even thought about what they would do to Samantha. What if they thought her sister was in on it too? Would they hurt her, or even worse, kill her? Kristen didn't want to think about that so she sparked up a blunt she had and waited for Amir to return.

Amir walked briskly to the planned meeting spot. The truck stop on 39th and Pershing would be full of people at this time and they could easily exchange the money. Raymond had been instructed to pass Amir the money and then he would be given directions where to find his niece. If Raymond hadn't known his people were on their way to rescue his daughter, he wouldn't have gone for that shit, but he knew in the end he was going to get his daughter and his money back.

As Amir slid in the booth across from Raymond, he sensed his anger and uncontrolled rage just below the surface, for some reason he felt the need to speak.

"She is not hurt."

Raymond just nodded his head, at this point it didn't matter, this nigga was dead regardless of the fact. Amir opened the duffle bag Raymond had given him under the table and couldn't help but to smile. He gave a nod and made a phone call. The next thing Raymond was being sent a text.

"Now remember if you follow us, you won't see her again, we are tracking your car." Amir lied. Raymond let him leave the restaurant first before he placed a call. It's done, give him time to get back to where he is going. I want them all dead within the hour."

Amir had called Timmo to let him know he had the cash and he was on his way back to the spot. Amir had initially thought it was crazy that Timmo was leading them to the safe house, but little did he know that is not what Timmo had in mind. He had sent the GPS coordinates to a place on the North side of Chicago. He wasn't foolish enough to lead them to her until he made his escape from Cook County.

Little did Timmo know, the twins soldier were taking position, surrounding the house and the block. There was no way Raymond planned to let any of those fools leave alive. When Charles saw the car that held Amir pulled up, he couldn't believe his eyes as Kristen got out of the passenger seat. He never would've guessed Samantha's little sister had helped to bring about the destruction of his family. She ate from the same plate as all of them. He made a note to holler at Samantha when this was over.

Taking what little they needed, Booman, Amir, Timmo and Kristen made their way out the back door to the alley. They had split the money and planned on going their separate ways. However, as soon as Booman stepped foot on the back porch, his body was lifted off the ground and lit up by what seemed like an endless amount of bullets, shortly after all hell broke loose.

"Oh shit, oh my God? What did I do?" Kristen cried out loud.

"Come on Kris, God can't save you now." Timmo said grabbing her and running through the alley. It seemed like every corner they turned, they were surrounded by gunfire. Kristen stopped.

"I can't do this Timmo, I can't make it, just go without me."

That wasn't an option for him, she knew too much and the only way she was getting left behind was with a bullet in her brain, and he still needed her, so he wasn't about to let that happen.

"You can do this Krissy, I love you and I got you." Timmo said looking her in the eye.

That gave Kristen the courage she needed, because she soon pulled herself together and began to run. She was right behind Timmo, trying to catch up when a shot rang out. Timmo stopped for a second when he no longer heard her breathing behind him. He saw her on the ground with blood pouring from her body. He left her dying in the alley and continued to get away.

Amir knew death was calling his name as he lay behind a garbage can bleeding from his abdomen. He would never get to enjoy his part of the three million dollars, but he wasn't going to go without taking a few people with him. He struggled to get up and aim his gun. H was able to let off two shots before he was hit in the back of the head by a bullet from Charles' gun.

Inside of the house, Mako rushed through the rooms calling Jaleesa's name. He knew she was there, where else could she be. Then he saw that the basement door was open. When he got down stairs, all he could do was hang his head. Jaleesa's body lay on the floor, still tied to the chair. She was bleeding from her head.

"Unc down here, down here!" He called to Terry. "Call the ambulance, she's been shot!"

Terry raced down the stairs an immediately called the ambulance when he saw Jaleesa, he doubted that she would make it, but he just hoped she could hold on. The ambulance arrived and took Jaleesa to the hospital. Her vital signs were low but she was still fighting, Mako just hoped she made it to the hospital where she would have a fighting chance.

"We're missing one of them." Al-G stated. "The nigga that started all the shit." He said giving Mako a hard look.

"Mako you need to get out of here. We don't need you anywhere near the scene, once the news crews get here. Mako nodded his head somberly. Mako couldn't believe that all this shit had happened. He had lost his best friend, and the woman he loved all in the same night. He should have known Timmo was going to do what he chose, but he never thought it would lead to this. Before he knew it Mako had jumped in his car and began driving. He didn't know where he was driving to until he pulled up in front of the ABLA Community Center in Timmo's old neighborhood, the Village. This is where it all started for him and Timmo. They had met on this very basketball court over fifteen years ago, and it was only fitting that this is where it ended.

Parking his car in the lot, he twisted a blunt and waited. For some reason, he just knew that Timmo would make the stop to his old neighborhood, before he fled the city with the cool million he had managed to get away with. Timmo hadn't wanted to leave in the first place and Mako had talked him into it. If he knew then what he knew now, Mako would have never suggested the idea. Mako never expected to fall in love with the niece of the men he was trying to destroy. He had definitely ever expected to be related to them in any way shape or form, but Mako had started this war and it was up to him to finish it.

Abraham had always told him to not start something he didn't plan on finishing. Unfortunately, the only way to finish this would end was in the death of his best friend. Charles had made himself very clear that it didn't matter if Abraham was Mako's grandfather, and his godfather. He would put a bullet in his brain if he didn't handle his business. Knowing he was the one at fault, he accepted his task with a heavy heart, but it was something that needed to be done.

Before Macon could contemplate anymore on how he ended up in a whirlwind of shit, a car pulled up and parked beside him. When he looked out the driver's side window, he saw it was Timmo. Mako's adrenaline kicked in with a rush of blood to his heart which was beating out of his chest. Timmo just smiles and rolled down his window.

"How did I know I would find you here?"

They both got out of their cars and walked to the ball court. Mako was nervous and anxious, but Timmo wasn't. He knew Mako had come to kill him, but he also knew Mako wasn't a killer. He had never put the murder game down a day in his life. He had always left tasks like that up to Timmo, claiming he couldn't afford to get his hands dirty for Abraham's sake. That didn't bother Timmo at all, he like the power he felt when he took the life of another man. Power like that was hard to come by in the streets. He knew Mako had come to kill him, and that is why he made sure to secure his Desert Eagle with the safety off when they got out of the car.

On the court, bathed by the street light, the two friends stared at each other in silence for a while, not knowing where to start. Mako spoke first.

"Why?"

"Why? Because you turned your back on me and left me in the cold. You ran back to your other life and said fuck me. As if all the moves we made in the streets together were for fun. It might have been a game for you rich boy, but that shit is my life!" Timmo laughed.

Mako was shocked by the venom he heard in Timmo's voice. Yeah, he may have come from money but throughout the years he made sure his best friend always made a come up when he did. Hell, he had funded their illegal schemes since the beginning, if he hadn't been rich, neither would Timmo.

"Because I decided to grow up and get out the game, you kidnap motherfuckers, and not just anybody, the niece of the men I told you were my family. That is betrayal, me warning you to stay clear of trouble."

"Warn me nigga? You told them fools we were coming and that is why they were ready for us!" Timmo spat.

Then it dawned on Mako, all this had been because Timmo thought he had betrayed him and given him up to the twins. In actuality, Mako had taken all the blame and never implicated Timmo, Booman, or Amir. He knew as soon as he spoke either of their names there would be a bounty on their heads, and he didn't want blood on his hands, especially not the blood of his best friend.

"Are you fucking kidding me?" Mako said.

"Naw nigga this ain't no joke. You think I don't know what you came down here to do?" Timmo said staring Mako down. "So man up and handle your business."

Before Macon knew what was happening Timmo had pulled out his Desert Eagle and had it pointed at Mako's chest. This was it. There would be no turning back now. The friendship was dead and one of them would be too. Before Mako knew it, his survival instinct kicked in and he had knocked the gun from Timmo's hand. They began fighting. Mako had always been a beast with his hands. He had fought many niggas in the hood for calling him rich boy, the only difference this time was that Timmo didn't have his back, he was trying to stab him in it.

Timmo regretted hesitating when pulling the trigger. He had never hesitated in his life. It was because the loyalty that he once felt for this nigga tripped him up. He knew Mako was a pro with those hands, which made him fight even harder to get to his gun that was lying just out of reach. Mako saw what he was reaching for and kicked the gun farther away. They both knew this would be a fight to the death, and neither one of them wanted to die. When Timmo got a lucky break and hit Mako square on the chin, he finally fell.

Out of breath, Timmo stood panting, watching Mako writhe on the ground in a daze from being hit on the chin. Walking over to him to finish the job, he wasn't expecting what happened next. Mako rolled over to his back, brought up the Desert Eagle and proceeded to fire off rounds hitting Timmo once in the shoulder and two times in the chest. Seeing the man who had once been his best friend fall to the ground in a pool of blood made Mako shudder. He had become a killer in the blink of an eye and his first killing had been one which involved betraying his brother. Realizing that he saw lights from the apartment windows opening and people peeking out of blinds, he quickly ditched the gun and fled the scene.

After Mako had peeled out, Timmo tried to sit himself up.

"Shit that hurt like a motherfucker." He said, staring at the wound in his shoulder.

Although Mako had hit him twice in the chest, the bullet proof vest he was wearing had saved his life. He started laughing when he thought how Little Cortez had given it to him. He didn't think he would need it knowing Mako didn't have the heart of a killer. Although he was pissed because his friend tried to kill him, he

209

couldn't help but be somewhat proud of the nigga that he had some heart.

Little Cortez slowly sat up in the backseat of Timmo's car. Timmo had brought him along knowing that he would need at least one soldier on his new journey. Little Cortez didn't have a home to speak of and was ecstatic when the boss chose him to flee with. Cortez had decided to lower the window to hear the heated discussion the friends were having. When he heard about the kidnapping and ransom, he knew what Timmo held in that black duffle bag in the trunk, more than a million dollars.

Cortez's mind was reeling at what he could do with a million dollars. All the hoes he could have and the shoes he would buy. Nobody would ever call him dusty again, and if this nigga Timmo would kill his best friend, what would he do to him when he no longer needed him? When Cortez heard Mako pull out of the lot he got out of the backseat of the car and went over to Timmo.

"Help me up shorty." Timmo said reaching out to take Cortez's hand.

Little Cortez didn't offer his hand back, and when Timmo looked into his eyes, he saw the eyes of a killer, one he helped to create. When Timmo saw him reaching for his gun he got up to try to run, but it was too late. Little Cortez sent two to the back of his dome. This was the second time Cortez had taken a life, but this one meant so much more than the first. He had killed a boss, which meant if he played his cards right all the power would be transferred to him. The 1.5 million sitting in the trunk of his new car would help pave the way.

The battle in the streets between the Johnson and Clark family may have died that night with Timmo, but in its wake, a new king had been born. One that was a renegade with no family or ties to anyone in the streets. A little nigga with nothing to lose, and nothing to live for, would prove to be a formidable opponent in the future for the Clark and Johnson families alike.

THE END

EPILOGUE

Juicy sat at Jaleesa's bedside as he had done every day for the last four weeks. She was still in a coma, the doctors said that it was the body's way of healing itself. No one knew if or when she would ever wake up. All Juicy could do was pray. The firsts and only date they'd had a few months ago had led them down a path he'd always wanted to go along with her. He couldn't believe that the day that he had actually built the courage to tell her how he truly felt, would end with her laying in a coma. He beat himself up constantly for not telling her sooner. His thoughts were interrupted by Raymond walking in the door. Juicy greeted him and could sense he wanted to be alone with Jaleesa, so he left out the room.

Raymond sat in the chair Juicy had vacated next to Jaleesa's bed. He took her hand in his and became chocked up when he went to speak.

"Baby girl, I need you to open your eyes. I have something important I need to tell you. Something I should have told you years ago, but my pride and promises stood in the way. It wasn't until I thought I had lost you that I found the courage to tell you."

Clearing his throat one more time, he bent down and whispered in her ear.

"Please wake up baby girl, Daddy misses you."

At that moment, Raymond swore he felt her squeeze his hand a little, but shook it off as his feelings getting the better of him. He dried his face with his free hand and looked at his daughter sleeping like a princess. All of a sudden, the monitors in her hospital room started beeping. Raymond was panicked getting up to push the nurses button, with his free hand he felt a slight tug on the hand that was holding Jaleesa's. When he looked down her eyes were fluttering open.

She was beginning to fully wake just as the nurses rushed into the room. She was trying to speak, but the tube down her throat made it hard.

"Take it out!" Raymond insisted. "She's trying to talk."

All this time Jaleesa had never once let his hand go and the very first word she had spoken in four weeks was, Daddy.

****

Tasha sat in the doctor's office nervously waiting on her test results. She didn't know what she really wanted the outcome to be at this appointment. Before she had a chance to ponder anything else she was called to the back room. After she sat down on the hard examining table, the doctor informed her that she was five weeks pregnant, and she fainted.

****

Little Cortez had hit the highway in Timmo's car after he left him dead at the court. He had never looked back at Chicago. He was leaving nothing behind, but bad ass memories. He was headed to Wisconsin, the land where nickel bags go for twenty and the clucks were gainfully employed. He didn't have his plan all together but he knew all that cash he was sitting on would make everything a little easier. Little Cortez was in a position where he could now be the boss and he planned to fill those shoes at all cost.

Made in the USA
Middletown, DE
19 May 2022